"This is your room," he said

Lauren tried to appear unmoved, as though the suite was nothing more nor less than she was accustomed to on a day-to-day basis. The place was *wonderful*!

"It seems...adequate." She made herself turn his way, and frowned. The intensity of his gaze had a surprising seductive quality. She dropped her gaze to Tina.

Her heart swelled, and she marveled at her good fortune to have stumbled into such an extraordinary opportunity—the chance to be with her niece, and to unmask Mr. Delacourte as utterly unfit to raise an innocent child.

"Come. I'll show you the baby's room." He glanced back, and with the quirk of a brow, added, "And you can show me how to change a diaper."

Her boss's suggestion finally penetrated. "Show you how to *what*?"

"Change a diaper. Is there a problem?"

Yes, there's a problem. I can't change a diaper! she cried mentally.

He crossed his arms and lounged against the wall, eyeing her with a furrowed brow. "If I am to raise this child, there are things I should know how to do...."

Dear Reader,

Back by popular request is our deliciously delightful series—**Baby Boom**. We've asked some of your favorite authors in Harlequin Romance® to bring you a few more special deliveries—of the baby kind!

Baby Boom is all about the true labor of love—parenthood and how to survive it! *The Billionaire Daddy* by Renee Roszel is this month's new arrival....

When two's company and three (or four...or five) is a family!

The Billionaire Daddy

Renee Roszel

BABY BOOM

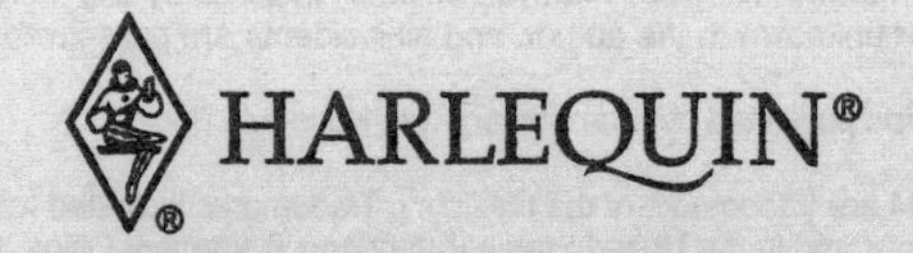

TORONTO • NEW YORK • LONDON
AMSTERDAM • PARIS • SYDNEY • HAMBURG
STOCKHOLM • ATHENS • TOKYO • MILAN • MADRID
PRAGUE • WARSAW • BUDAPEST • AUCKLAND

To Norman V. Roszel
and
Randall Albert Roszel
You are much missed

ISBN 0-373-03589-6

THE BILLIONAIRE DADDY

First North American Publication 2000.

This edition published by arrangement with Harlequin Books S.A.

Visit us at www.romance.net

Printed in U.S.A.

PROLOGUE

DADE DELACOURTE scowled at the tiny infant wrapped in pink. As the nurse wheeled the bassinet to the viewing window for his inspection, the baby slept on, innocently oblivious to his anger and shock. Dade's narrowed gaze moved to a card, taped to the newborn's bed. Baby Girl Delacourte was boldly printed there for all of New York City to see.

He peered at the tiny bundle, then glanced at the picture he'd been handed. His image smiled up at him from the glossy print. Wrapped in his possessive embrace was a beautiful, smiling blonde.

Flipping the picture over, he read the scribbled writing. "Dade and Millie. It's love!" Below that declaration was the date, March 15 of last year. The baby had been born yesterday, December 15. Nine months to the day...

He flicked his glance to the child. Sometime during the night, the newborn's mother had slipped unnoticed from the hospital. Before her disappearance, however, she'd listed Dade Delacourte as the child's father on the birth certificate. Her coup de grâce had been this picture she'd left behind, a telling testament to Dade's paternity.

The situation was all very cut-and-dried. The mother, Millicent "Smith" had abandoned her child. Dade, the father of record, would necessarily take custody.

There was only one small hitch in the scenario. *Dade had never seen this woman before in his life.*

But saying so would repair nothing, either legally or morally. He eyed the fidgety hospital administrator and gave a curt nod. "Naturally I'll pay the bill." He crumpled the photo in his fist. "The child is mine."

CHAPTER ONE

Nearly six months later

LAUREN SMITH knew she was crazy. A sane woman wouldn't burst into the lobby of a swanky Manhattan high rise, all marble and crystal and gold. Not a sane woman wearing a bargain basement shift and carrying a battered canvas suitcase. Yet, even as deranged as she was, she realized she was a far cry from the type who belonged in these surroundings.

Since her sanity was no longer a consideration, she might as well forge on, figure out a way to dredge up the nerve to force a confrontation with the rich and powerful scoundrel who occupied the penthouse.

"You will go up to that fancy doorman and demand entry." She stiff-armed the revolving door. The uniformed sentry eyed her with mistrust. She swallowed. "Don't let him see your fear," she muttered. "Tell him you'll chain yourself to—to..." She gave the cavernous, glittering lobby a panicked examination. "To what? *With* what?"

Plan B.

She yanked back her shoulders and marched toward the scowling watchdog in his fancy epaulets and frippery. "Make him understand this is a matter of life and death," she muttered under her breath. She eyed the man with bloodthirsty resolve. *"His!"*

The guard opened his mouth, but she cut him off.

"I must see Mr. Dade Delacourte immediately, on a matter of—"

"It's about time!" He grasped her elbow and whirled her toward a bank of gilded elevators. "Get up there, girl!" He turned a key in a slot above the buttons marking the building's eighty floors. "Mr. Delacourte is roaring like a wounded lion."

Before she could demand or threaten or even breathe, Lauren found herself shooting upward. She grabbed the rail to avoid staggering to her knees, no longer curious about how it felt to be blasted into space. Dazed, she watched the floors zoom by—35-48-67... After soaring past eighty, the elevator kept going, though the space where the numbers had been displayed went ominously blank. "Where does this guy live?" She strangled the handrail, suddenly panicked. "Pluto?"

The rocketing conveyance came to a stop so smooth Lauren decided the engineering required for such a soft landing could be afforded only by the filthy rich. She had been so tense in her attempt to keep from crashing through the roof, she nearly fell backward from overcompensation. Lauren shook her head, working to focus on a world no longer falling away at the speed of light. The elevator doors whooshed open.

She stilled, hardly breathing, to take in the unknown—this alien, celestial region called "a penthouse."

A spacious foyer appeared before her, with lush carpeting and white marble walls, luxurious yet austere. On either side of a set of double doors gray stone pedestals supported imposing earthenware urns, no doubt exhumed from some primal civilization. Lauren would bet her teacher's pension they were priceless.

She heard a sound and shifted in time to see a woman in starched gray push open the double doors and rush toward her. "Hurry, hurry!" She beckoned, her gestures nervous, impatient. "He's waiting."

Lauren tentatively stepped out of the elevator. The heels of her pumps burrowed into the thick carpet, and she swayed precariously. In the process of righting herself, she realized she still held her suitcase. She hadn't even had time to find a hotel, having rushed immediately to the Delacourte building.

She wondered if she should leave the bag by the elevator. Her quandary was cut short when it was snatched away. "I'll get this into the limo," the woman whispered. "Just *go!*" Before Lauren could get steady on her feet, she felt a hand at her back, then a brisk shove. "It's the second door on your left, after you leave the foyer."

Her equilibrium returning, Lauren twisted to ask what in heaven's name the woman was talking about, and what was behind the second door to the left after the foyer. "But—" She cut herself off, dismayed to see the maid disappear behind the closing elevator doors.

Lauren would have been relieved by such a frenzied reception, except for the fact that nobody knew she was coming. She wanted nothing more than to have Mr. Delacourte relinquish her baby niece with speed and enthusiasm. Unfortunately he had no idea Lauren Smith existed. He didn't know her little sister had been the woman who had given birth to his child.

Even if he didn't want the baby—which she was sure he didn't, having left Millie alone and pregnant—he could have no idea who Lauren was or the reason she'd come to New York City. So, why had she been rushed up to his penthouse as though she were a fireman and the place was a blazing inferno?

Nervously she peered beyond open double doors, twenty feet straight ahead. She saw a long hallway that opened into what no doubt was the living room. Eyeing the second door on the left in the hall, she chewed her lower lip. Assuming the "he" the maid mentioned was Dade Delacourte, she should stomp right in and state her business.

She would have her chance to explain who she was, and make it clear she had no intention of allowing him to be burdened with a baby he didn't want. She had come to take little Christina Lauren Delacourte off his depraved hands.

She fought a shiver of loathing. *No! Don't call him depraved!* She must be civil. Just because he'd lied to Millie, and told her he could get her into movies, seduced her, then dumped her was no reason to be nasty. Just because his little fling had left Millie pregnant, with no place to go but home to Oklahoma and Lauren, was no excuse to walk in and kick him in the shins. Though the idea had a certain merit. He probably wanted to get rid of the baby as much as she wanted custody. They could handle this in a rational, adult manner.

Lauren heard a click and glanced up in time to see a tall man wearing beige slacks and a navy knit shirt. As he exited the second doorway to the left, he raked a hand through hair, dark as midnight. "Dammit," he growled, making her flinch. "Where is that nanny? She was supposed to be on her way up..." He turned. His gaze clashed with hers. *"You!"* The word sounded like an accusation, and Lauren took an unsteady step backward. "You're the nanny the agency sent."

His narrowed glare cut off her ability to breathe.

Muscles bunched in his jaw. "Don't dawdle, woman!" He flicked a hand in a gesture that she follow him. "Come see to the child. We were supposed to leave for the Hamptons over an hour ago."

With a quick snap of broad shoulders he pivoted away. She stared, struck by a purposeful, stalking grace to his movements, a man clearly in control of his world. Lauren realized instantly who this growling scoundrel was. She'd done research on him once the private detective she'd hired finally discovered where Millie had run off to, just before the baby was due.

It had taken the investigator nearly six months, but yesterday he'd called with news. Millie—bitter and bent on revenge—had hitchhiked to New York City, where she'd given birth to a baby girl, Christina Lauren Delacourte, listing Dade Delacourte on the birth certificate as the father. Her retaliation for being abandoned by him, had been to abandon her child *to* him, to raise, alone.

For a woman like Millie, selfish to the core, forcing Mr. Delacourte into years and years of parental responsibility was the perfect payback. Then she'd silently slipped away, no doubt back in Hollywood, using some stage name as she followed her single-minded dream to become a movie star.

As Lauren stared after Mr. Delacourte, she gritted her teeth, telling herself sternly that he was *not* all that handsome. Yet, even as she struggled to believe that, she took a step in his direction, then another, some part of her responding without the authorization of her brain.

You're the nanny the agency sent.

Come see to the child.

The jumble of words echoed in her dazed brain. *You're the nanny the agency sent. Come see to the child.* As the fog of panic and confusion began to clear, she went over those two sentences again, with more understanding. *You're the nanny the agency sent! Come see to the child!*

He thought she was a nanny? Did he think he'd hired *her* to take care of his baby? Her niece? *Her own little namesake?* She blinked, focusing on his broad back as she absorbed this turn of events.

He reached another door and shifted to look back. His brows dipped ominously when he saw she hadn't ventured beyond the foyer. "Miss Quinn, if you're having second thoughts about this job, say so. I don't have time to read your mind."

His admonition jarred her out of her stupor. Miss Quinn? So that was the nanny's name. Hadn't he said he was planning to leave for the Hamptons? An hour ago! No doubt he needed a nanny to keep the "little nuisance" out of his way while he hosted wild parties on his private beach.

A stab of renewed disgust made her recoil. *Oh, no,* she vowed, *little Christina Lauren won't be tainted by the immoral lifestyle of this beast—not if she had her way!*

The words of the lawyer she'd consulted came back, cracking like a whip in her brain. "Miss Smith, if Mr. Delacourte is *not* inclined to give over custody, no court in the land is likely to take his child away from him. He's the CEO of the multibillion dollar

Delacourte Industries, a highly respected man. The only way you could get custodianship of your niece would be to uncover damning evidence against him. *Prove* he is an unfit parent."

Icy dread twisted in her stomach. What if he said no to her request, and tossed her out on her ear! She couldn't stand the thought, couldn't bear to go back to Oklahoma without Christina. Just imagining it shattered her.

On the other hand, there was no question that Dade Delacourte was a lecher. Poor Millie was a living example of his reckless lust. All Lauren would need to get proof of his utter lack of suitability to bring up an innocent little girl was to spend a few days in close proximity with the man. That would provide her with all the proof she would need. But how—

The two sentences he'd shouted at her came roaring back. *You're the nanny the agency sent. Come see to the child.*

Her brain exploded with a profound insight. A *nanny* would spend time in close proximity with him—under the same roof! Here was her chance! Providence had dropped it right in her lap! Did she dare refuse?

"Well?" he growled, and she jumped.

"I—I'm coming—sir." *If proof of Mr. Delacourte's unfitness is what it will take to get my niece, then I'll get it, or my name isn't Lauren Smith!* Which, ironically, right now it wasn't. Since she planned to make every effort to insure that Mr. Delacourte *believed* she was Miss Something Quinn.

Trying not to think about how foolhardy this slapdash scheme might be, Lauren put one foot in front of the other, increasing her pace, scurrying down the long hallway toward the man she most despised in the world.

She sent up a prayer that Miss Quinn wouldn't show up now to blow her cover. Since the woman was this late, and since Mr. Delacourte didn't exactly live in an out-of-the-way hovel, it seemed that for whatever reason, Miss Quinn—*the thoughtful, marvelous no-show Miss Quinn*—wasn't coming.

Mr. Delacourte turned the knob and looked inside. "Opal, Miss Quinn is here. Once she sees to the child's last-minute needs, show them to the car."

When Lauren joined Mr. Delacourte at the nursery entrance, he faced her. "Most of the baby's things are already in the limo, and she's been fed."

Before Lauren could respond, he was striding away. "We're leaving in fifteen minutes."

He disappeared behind another door, but Lauren continued to gape after him. "Yes, Your Majesty," she muttered, her hostility for the egotistical tyrant bubbling to the surface.

"Miss?"

The female voice startled Lauren, and she spun around. The nursery, furnished with a crib, built-ins and a changing table, held all the whimsy of a hospital room. Everything was white, except the inside of the crib. Its head and footboards were painted in a vivid palate of pastels. A mobile of dangling miniature teddy bears hung above the mattress, its sheets adorned with cartoon characters. The crib was a colorful oasis amid a scrubbed wilderness of white.

A rosy-cheeked woman in gray smiled when Lauren's glance met hers. The middle-aged maid cuddled a frilly, pink bundle to her breast. One tiny hand reached up and grasped the woman's chin, causing her to chuckle. "Tina, sugar-baby, meet your new nanny."

Lauren's heart did a flip-flop. *Tina!* Her niece was right there in the same room, not ten feet away! It was a miracle. This morning she'd stepped off the plane from Tulsa, and gone directly to Delacourte Industry headquarters. She'd been refused an appointment, stiffly informed the CEO would be away for a month. Her hopes had plummeted into the black depths of gloom. This rash cab ride to his Manhattan apartment had been an act of desperation. She'd had no idea—not even the flicker of a dream—that…

She shook herself. Why was she standing there like a frozen fish stick? With a fledgling smile she fairly floated across the room to gaze down at her niece. Lauren's parents were dead and Millie had disappeared into the world of wanna-be movie stars. So, it was imperative to Lauren not to lose Christina.

As she stared at the tiny face, the tingle of threatening tears made her blink. "Such an angel," she murmured. Her joy so overwhelmed her, it took monumental effort to keep from sobbing.

"She's so sweet." The maid handed Lauren the swaddled child. "Hardly ever cries. Sally, the other nanny, said caring for this sugar-baby was the most enjoyable job she's ever had. But you know hormones."

Lauren only half listened, her heart spilling over with a love that was almost maternal. She gently held Tina in her arms, taking in every detail, from the pale, blond wisps of her hair to her precious, heart-shaped mouth. Something in the maid's chatter caught her attention and she looked up. "Hormones?"

Opal tittered. "No matter how much Sally loved

and doted on little Tina, her hormones won out. She ran off with the night doorman sometime before dawn this morning. Said in her note she couldn't bear to be separated from the guy for a whole month.'' Opal shook her head, smoothing a strand of graying hair into her chignon. ''Why do so many women turn into drooling idiots when it comes to a smooth-talking man?''

Lauren found the statement ironic. Opal was talking about the night doorman, but she could have been referring to Mr. Delacourte's effect on Millie. ''Whatever the reason, there's a lot of that going around,'' Lauren said with a sad shake of her head.

Opal laughed and nodded. ''Ain't it the truth! Ain't it the truth.'' She gave Tina a pat on her chubby cheek. ''You have yourself a great time out there on the beach, little one.'' Looking at Lauren, she waved toward a stuffed, leather bag. ''I think I've got everything in there she'll need for the trip—bottles, diapers and such. You'd best check her to see if she needs changing before you go.''

She lay a hand on the crib headboard, drawing Lauren's gaze to it again. Upon closer inspection she noticed the painting was more than mere swirls of color, but seemed truly like art. ''Who painted the crib?'' she asked, surprised to hear herself speaking aloud.

Opal gave the crib a quick glance, then looked back at Lauren. ''Oh, Benny did that while Tina was still sleeping in her bassinet. Benny's Cook's assistant, and quite a budding artist.'' She laughed. ''The whole staff's so crazy about Tina. Poor dear child hardly gets any time to sleep, with somebody wanting to rock her and cuddle her all the time.'' She checked her wristwatch. "Oh, goodness. Time's flying. Yell out when you're ready. I'll be down the hall."

After Opal left, Lauren stood for a long minute, gazing at her precious niece. "No problem," she finally murmured, but it came out sounding dubious. The full weight of what she'd done was settling in.

She would be living with a man she hated—spying on him—and even more disturbing than that, the well-being of an infant, not quite six months old, was in her hands!

Hysteria welled up inside her. *What had she done?* Being a high school music teacher hadn't exactly qualified her for digging up incriminating evidence on wild living playboys. Not to mention one other tiny detail. Though Lauren had done plenty of baby-sitting, and loved children, she'd never cared for actual *babies!* "Oh, Lauren," she mumbled, "what have you gotten yourself into?"

Dade and his new nanny sped along the highway toward the Hamptons in his luxurious silver limousine. As he spoke on his cell phone to his secretary, leaving last-minute instructions, he glanced at his new employee. She sat stiffly in the forward seating area, which faced the back seat where he was positioned. The arrangement accommodated more comfortable conversation. He half grinned at the thought, since his new nanny had not only said nothing, she hadn't even made eye contact. It seemed she had no interest in anything or anyone but the baby.

What was her name, again? Miss Something Quinn. Was it Nelda or Gilda Quinn? He couldn't recall what the agency told him. He'd been in a foul mood at the time, so her given name had hardly been his main concern.

His business calls finally concluded, Dade slipped the phone into his slacks pocket. He surveyed the nanny as she gazed at Tina, secured in her car seat. The nanny had the strangest expression on her face. It looked like adoration. He lounged back, straightening his legs and crossing them at the ankles. His shoes almost touched her, but she paid him absolutely no heed, just kept gazing at Tina.

He supposed nannies—at least the really good ones—adored children. He'd certainly had good luck with the other nanny—until this morning. He cleared his throat to get his new nanny's attention.

Nothing.

It irritated him that she ignored him so completely. She hadn't even acknowledged him with a glance when Goodberry helped her into the car. Such total lack of notice didn't happen to him. People came to attention in his presence, skittering around, catering to his every whim. Wealth and power had that effect on people. Especially people whose livelihoods depended on his approval.

In the eleven years since he'd taken over his father's electronics business, he'd turned it into a multibillion dollar corporation, no small part of that success due to several of his own patents. He'd learned to take for granted that his vice presidents would snap to attention when he cleared his throat. So why couldn't this wisp of a woman oblige him by at least glancing to see if he was choking to death.

She made a cooing sound and stuck a finger against the baby's palm. When Tina grasped it, Miss Quinn smiled. Dade dipped his head slightly to get a better look. Were her eyes swimming with tears? He frowned. Tears? Perhaps the woman had allergies, or was in the weepy part of her cycle. She couldn't be that overcome by having a baby grasp her finger. Or maybe she could. Nannies were most likely a very sentimental breed when it came to their charges.

He cleared his throat again. Seconds ticked by while he felt the ignominy of being scorned. He counseled with himself, *Dade, buddy, I hope you haven't become a pompous ass, expecting the world to revolve around you.*

Her lack of attentiveness irked him. After all, the woman worked for him. She owed him the courtesy of acknowledging that he existed on the face of the earth! He scanned her from head to toe. She was pleasant looking, in a sensible-shoes way. Her brown hair was cropped to just above shoulder length in a straight, no-nonsense style. Her eyes were a no-nonsense olive-drab, and her lips had spent most of their time in his presence pressed together in a no-nonsense grimace.

Only now, with the baby, had he seen her smile. The sunny expression turned her cheeks a fetching pink and brought a radiance to her eyes that gave them a whole other dimension. A mossy green, soft and lush. The combination of her no-nonsense demeanor, plus her visible softness where Tina was concerned, pleased him, even if she did ignore him with what seemed like a very real desire to have him disappear.

He grinned to himself at the ridiculous thought. This was a well-paying job, and cushy as jobs went. She had no reason to dislike him. He decided to give up on subtle, and take the direct approach. "Miss

Quinn?'' He paused, with no intention of going on until she acknowledged him.

She didn't make a single move to let him know she'd heard. He pursed his lips with annoyance.

''Miss Quinn, do you have a hearing problem?'' he asked, more loudly.

Her glance flicked his way, though she didn't quite meet his eyes, more like his cheek. ''Oh, uh, no. I can hear.''

He crossed his arms before him. ''Don't you think, when your employer speaks to you, it would be polite to answer?''

Her no-nonsense face paled, and her brows quirked downward. ''I didn't—I mean...'' When she met his gaze, tiny lightning bolts of unease flickered in her eyes. ''Yes, sir.'' She inclined her head, and Dade thought she was going to look at the baby. Instead, she watched him from beneath her lashes, like a feral cat peering out from the underbrush.

Lord, what was that look? Fear? Hate? He couldn't tell if she was about to faint or attack. *Attack?* He grinned wryly at the crazy notion, concluding he knew what was wrong. He'd been a brute when she arrived, and she was afraid of him. He damned himself for his churlishness. She probably thought he was an ogre to be avoided at all costs.

In an effort to make amends, he decided light conversation was in order. After all, they would be living together. He didn't want her to pass out every time he spoke to her. ''What's your first name, Miss Quinn?'' he asked.

A flash of discomfort skidded over her features, and Dade wondered why the question might cause her trouble. He'd taken care to use his most diplomatic tone.

"I—" She swallowed and lifted her chin a notch. "I prefer Miss Quinn, sir. Or just Quinn."

Her cool reply surprised him. He observed her silently for a moment, experiencing a mixture of amusement and exasperation. With a quirk of his lips, he nodded. "Okay, Just Quinn. Call me Dade."

She didn't smile, merely lowered her gaze to the baby. "No, thank you, sir."

No, thank you, sir?

With a quizzical lift of a brow, he watched her features change from frosty to sweet as she gazed at the baby.

He didn't recall a time when he'd felt so thoroughly dismissed. It appeared that the truly proficient nannies of the world felt superior, a bit arrogant, being in such demand. Not particularly familiar with nannies himself, their pecking order was new to him. Even if the agency hadn't faxed him her résumé, Miss Quinn's haughtiness alone had to mean she was one hell of a nanny.

Or maybe she simply hid her anxiety better than most. Some people defended themselves with belligerence. He decided to try again to develop a rapport. Perhaps a compliment. "You don't look thirty-seven, Quinn," he said. "I wouldn't have guessed you are even thirty."

She flicked him a wary glance. The smile he offered her was so courteous he could have been poster boy for the Kindly Scouts of America.

"I consider flattery a brother to sexual harassment, sir. How old I look is irrelevant to my position as nanny."

He was caught off guard by her prickly rejoinder, his only response the astonished lift of one eyebrow. She had spunk. He had to give her that. But if she thought her lame threat would fly in his town, she was a little naive for thirty-seven.

Not one to give up easily, he decided to try again. "Tina's a very good baby, Miss Quinn. My other nanny said so a thousand times."

She cast him an oddly petulant look but didn't reply. "I haven't had much spare time to be with Tina, myself." He paused, deciding she didn't need to know he'd been busy trying to reorient his life to accommodate a child he'd neither expected nor wanted. Now that he'd finally worked out the necessary business adjustments, this month in the Hamptons would be the second, most difficult phase. Learning how to be a "father."

"Will you be wanting weekly reports on her status, sir?" she asked, breaking through his thoughts. "Or bimonthly?"

"What?" He had no idea what reports she could mean. "I don't—" His cell phone rang. With a halting lift of his hand, he excused himself, fishing the phone from his trouser pocket.

Lauren cringed at the memory of Mr. Delacourte's shocked expression when she'd made her "sexual harassment" remark. He'd been taken by surprise. Clearly the *last* thing on his mind was flattery. He was making conversation, his motives not even vaguely sinful. Why that realization disconcerted her, she had no idea. She was not there to be flattered by the man, she was there to show him up for the irresponsible impregnator of women he was.

Troubled, she surveyed the posh interior of the limousine. It wasn't huge, like those stretch limo's she'd seen in movies. It was only slightly bigger than a regular luxury car. The major difference she could see was that the white leather seats faced each other. This arrangement unsettled her, since she would have preferred not to see *him* every time she looked up.

Tina had fallen asleep, so Lauren continued to scan the interior, trying to concentrate on anything other than the annoying man with his long legs casually stretched out before her. She hadn't been able to help notice how the cotton trousers showed off nice thighs and well-developed calves. *Nice thighs and well-developed—*

She wasn't doing a very good job of shifting her thoughts. She groaned. She sensed he heard and shot an apprehensive glance in his direction. He peered at her and covered the receiver. "Something wrong?"

She shook her head, compelling her glance to the hand-rubbed teak consoles, the CD and videocassette player. Even a color TV! She sighed. Lolling her head against the soft leather, she looked heavenward. Bright sky through the moon roof pierced her eyes and made her wince. Emotions frayed to the breaking point, she squeezed her eyes shut.

With a calming inhale, she recalled the man who'd assisted her into the car. In his late fifties, he'd impressed her as being kind. That surprised her. She'd assumed a man like Dade Delacourte would have a driver who looked more sinister. Of course, looks could be deceiving. She'd only seen the driver for a moment as he'd opened the door for her. He'd been as courtly as a footman helping a princess into her carriage.

A glass partition behind her separated them from the man. She thought about turning to check out the front seat of the car, but she didn't shift around. She didn't dare appear too much like a gawking hayseed. Surely Miss Quinn had been in limousines before and took them for granted.

She recrossed her legs, catching a glimpse of the luxury carpet. It was pristine white, as though it had never had a foot set on it until today. Regrettably, also residing on that snow-white carpet—much too close—was a pair of size twelve tan suede bucks attached to well-developed calves and...

This time she managed to stifle her groan. So he was good-looking! So what! What had she expected? The man was a seduction machine! She knew that already, so why was she surprised to find out that a seduction machine would most likely be seductive! Even when he wasn't trying.

Rich laughter drew her gaze to his face and she made an involuntary examination of his features. The car's halo lighting reflected in his gray eyes, kindling them with dazzling beauty. His straight forehead and aquiline nose were the sort of features women would stand in line for days to behold, not to mention that chin, square and slashed with a sexy cleft. She grew peevish and unhappy with herself for finding anything about him appealing. He was a lecherous weasel.

She threw him a withering glare, but he was too preoccupied with his conversation to notice.

She hoped, in the next few days, she could catch him knee deep in debauchery. Spending too much time around Mr. Dade Delacourte-of-the-pretty-boy-charm-and-complete-lack-of-scruples was a dangerous idea—and not just for the baby.

CHAPTER TWO

LAUREN didn't know what she expected to see when they arrived at Dade Delacourte's seaside home. The Hampton's palatial estates were referred to ironically as "cottages," though they bore as much resemblance to a cottage as a pencil resembled a computer.

Lauren supposed she expected a billionaire playboy to vacation in ostentatious, even tacky, luxury. She wouldn't be surprised if the River Styx flowed right outside a twenty-foot, flaming gate. With this inflammatory vision in her head, Lauren was startled when Goodberry turned the limo onto a narrow, wooded lane marked by nothing more than a small metal sign reading Private Property. Perhaps the infamous river hid somewhere within the deceptively inviting forest of weathered pine and oak trees.

She frowned, staring out the window, trying to catch any glimpse. They emerged from the peaceful woodland, and Lauren was taken aback. She witnessed no fiery gateway. The pine-scented air held no hint of brimstone. Instead Lauren saw a wonderful house, more the image of a picturesque Vermont barn than a palatial mansion. Constructed of antique barn siding and stone, the home sprawled within an unpretentious, natural setting. Even from where Lauren sat, the bluff commanded a panoramic view of the Atlantic.

"Miss Quinn? Are you all right?"

Mr. Delacourte's question yanked Lauren from her

musings. She could tell he had raised his voice, so it was embarrassingly clear he'd been trying to get her attention. She glanced at him. "Yes, sir? I mean, yes, I'm fine."

He watched her quizzically for another moment, as though it crossed his mind that she was more astonished by the house than a nanny of her qualifications and job history should be. "Quinn, if you'll get the baby, I'll show you to your room."

Goodberry opened their door, and Mr. Delacourte flicked a glance at the driver. "The oceanfront guest suite has been prepared for Quinn and the child."

"Yes, sir." Goodberry stepped forward, offering Lauren a hand and smile. "May I help you, miss?"

The servant was so old-world gallant, Lauren couldn't keep from smiling. "Why thank you, Goodberry." She mused again about how sweet the driver was, and stole a quick look at her unprincipled employer.

Mr. Delacourte watched her with that same quizzical stare. Snapping her gaze away, she unbuckled Tina from her car seat and allowed Goodberry to assist them out of the limo.

Once safely out of the car, Lauren approached the stone walk meandering from the driveway of crushed seashells. There was no real lawn, just the grasses and low flowering vegetation that grew naturally in the sandy soil. Trees lined the walk and dotted the yard, enhancing the unaffected charm of the residence.

Lauren felt a hand at her elbow and jumped.

"It's only me," Mr. Delacourte said. "I thought it would be easier to guide you to your room. Besides, the path is a little uneven. We wouldn't want you falling."

She cast him a black glance. Was this a come-on, already? Did he "initiate" young, female help with a quick seduction on the first night? She jerked from his hold. She certainly had no plans to follow in her sister's footsteps. "I don't believe in physical contact between employer and employee, sir." Jutting her chin, she focused on the front door, which was up several steps, across a broad, covered stone porch. "Why don't you walk in front of me? I don't think the baby and I will get lost."

He cleared his throat and Lauren wondered if she heard a hint of amusement, as though he were hiding a chuckle. "Forgive me, Quinn. I'll watch my hands very carefully in the future." He bounded up the steps and proceeded to open the door. "Would you care to go inside, first?" He canted his head in query. "If I promise not to touch?"

His eyes sparkled, even in the shade of the porch. Lauren felt a prickle of irritation. He was laughing at her! As though it was just *too* funny that she thought, even for an instant, that he had anything more sexy in mind than to make sure she didn't break an ankle and sue his pants off. Apparently that was the only way she might get Mr. Delacourte out of his pants.

So much for his seducing every female employee. She was definitely not on his I-must-have-her-tonight list. She gritted her teeth, wishing she could be sure she wasn't blushing. The fact that her face burned was a bad sign. Scurrying inside, she concentrated on Tina and her sweet smile. The innocence of the sight helped calm her nerves.

"Please follow me, Quinn," Mr. Delacourte said. She nodded, but refused to meet his gaze. She knew her cheeks were flushed, and she didn't believe seeing amusement in his eyes would do anything to improve that situation.

Instead she glanced around. The great room looked as though it had been built around a real eighteenth century barn. The ceiling had to be thirty feet high, with thick beams of weathered pine supporting a steeply pitched roof. The floor was stone, the walls, old barn siding. A window-wall took up much of the ocean side of the house, with breathtaking views of surf, sand and sky.

Lauren was impressed, not so much by the fact that her boss had the wealth to own a coveted chunk of Long Island seacoast, but that his estate was more homey then she expected. *Nevertheless,* she counseled inwardly, *Dade Delacourte doesn't have to live in a golden villa in Sodom or Gomorrah to be a thrill-seeking-woman-chaser!*

Lauren trailed a limousine's length behind Mr. Delacourte, yet didn't lose sight of him as he exited the great room and headed down a hallway. His soft-soled shoes made hardly a sound on the wide pine planks.

Lauren passed a kitchen brimming with sunlight, lush green plants and the delectable scents of cooking food. She got a quick glimpse of a woman bustling around amid pots and pans, but only a glimpse. It appeared Mr. Delacourte wasn't inclined to make introductions.

"This is your room, Quinn," he said, halting at a sunlit entrance. "It's actually two rooms. The small one off to the left has been set up as the nursery. If there's anything you lack, please tell Goodberry or Braga, the cook."

Lauren tried to appear unmoved, as though the

suite was nothing more nor less than she was accustomed to on a day-to-day basis. But, heavenly days, the place was wonderful! It had the idyllic grace of a rural cabin, but with the view of a palace. The furnishings were a mix of antique and contemporary, of warm woods and wicker and bright, sunny hues.

On one wall of coarse siding, a collection of old weather vanes gave a sense of drama and fantasy to the room. A shaker rocker sat before the French doors, giving the open space a welcoming, country porch feel. Frothy sheers puddled at the outermost reaches of the glass doors, looking as though they were there for show, never really employed to obscure visual access to the grassy dunes, beach and sparkling sea.

"Miss Quinn?"

His stern use of her name relayed, once again, that he was afraid she'd fallen into some peculiar brain fog. Which she had. Lauren blinked several times, hoping the small flutter of lashes wouldn't alert Mr. Delacourte to the fact that she'd been deeply intent on computing the pros and cons of the place. "It seems—adequate."

She made herself turn his way, and frowned. The intensity of his gaze had a surprising seductive quality, and she felt awkward and uncertain. "I—I'll make a thorough survey, however—to be sure I have everything Tina and I require." Deciding the situation was making her feel awkward and uncertain enough without staring into his watchful eyes, she dropped her gaze to Tina.

Her heart swelled, and she could hardly keep her happiness locked inside. Lauren marveled at her good fortune to have stumbled into such an extraordinary opportunity—the chance to be with her niece, *and* to unmask Mr. Delacourte as utterly unfit to raise an innocent little girl.

"Come." He moved into the room, his scent pleasantly filling her nostrils as he passed her in the doorway. She noticed he took care not to touch her. "I'll show you the baby's room." He glanced back, and with the quirk of a brow, added, "And none too soon. If I'm not mistaken, that expression on her face means she's—occupied."

Lauren didn't understand, and glanced at the baby. Her face was screwed up as though she were having a very deep thought. Chubby cheeks were flushed red. What in the world could that possibly mean— Suddenly Lauren detected a scent much less pleasant than Dade's aftershave. *Oh!*

"This is good timing," Mr. Delacourte said. "You can show me how to change a diaper."

Lauren heard his words, though they didn't quite penetrate. Her brain was occupied by this new problem, one that forced her to realize she hadn't thought her plan through. She had *never* changed a diaper. She took a breath, then was sorry she had. "Tina, honey," she murmured, "for a sweet little darling, you..." Her boss's suggestion finally penetrated, and she shot a glance toward him. "Show you how to *what?*" She flinched at the panicked edge to the question.

He had reached the door to the baby's room and turned, his expression concerned. "I said you could show me how to change a diaper. Is there a problem?"

Yes, there's a problem! I can't change a diaper! she cried mentally, searching in her mind for what to actually say to the man. "You—you want me to show you how to change a diaper?"

He crossed his arms and lounged against the wall, eyeing her with a wrinkled brow. "If I am to raise this child, there are things I should know how to do."

"But that's what a nanny is for." She didn't want him watching her beginning, fumbling efforts at taking care of a baby. "You—you leave it to me."

His jaw worked, and Lauren could tell he was no more happy about this than she. "No. I've decided I..." He halted, his nostrils flaring. "Your job description does not include an expectation that I explain my motives, Quinn." He indicated the way with a curt nod. "If you don't mind?"

I mind! I really, really mind! she shrieked telepathically, barely managing to keep her features unruffled. With a slow, delaying nod, she trudged toward the nursery. She tried to calm herself. How hard could it be? She'd seen babies being diapered in TV ads. You simply take one of those disposables out of the box, place the baby's backside on it, slip the part that goes in front between her legs and fasten it with the adhesive tabs. Any idiot with the IQ of sawdust could do that!

The nursery didn't get much notice. Lauren had the impression it was similarly rustic to her room, though the furniture was white with pink accessories and there weren't any weather vanes on the walls.

She spied the flat surface and assumed this was where she was to change the baby, mainly because Mr. Delacourte had moved to stand beside it. She scanned the plastic covered countertop. To her horror, she spied beneath it a shelf heaped with cloth diapers, folded in squares. *Cloth?* She'd never seen a commercial where anybody folded a cloth diaper! She didn't even know cloth diapers were sold anymore.

"Cloth?" she asked, her voice quivering slightly.

"The environment needs all the help it can get."

She peered at him, forcing herself not to shout, *So you torture me instead!* Pressing her lips between her teeth, she nodded as anger flared. He supposedly cared about the environment, but he didn't care about the women he impregnated on his overnight dalliances! "It's nice to know you have a conscience about some things," she muttered.

"Excuse me?"

She cringed. Had she said that out loud? "I said—" she stalled "—it's nice to know you have a conscience about these things."

His low laughter was rich. "Thank you, Quinn. I'll try not to be too wounded by your astonishment."

With clamped jaws, she gingerly lay Tina on the changing surface. "I'm sure you'll heal, sir." She busied herself unsnapping Tina's pink romper, trying to look as though she knew what she was doing. Considering the fact that she was frightened to death, she was amazed and gratified to notice her fingers hardly shook.

Tina seemed so fragile. She didn't want to break any tiny arms or legs or fingers or toes. As she meticulously worked her way toward diaper removal, Mr. Delacourte hovered at her elbow. Though he'd vowed not to touch, as she maneuvered, she brushed his belly and chest with her arm. He didn't shift away. She supposed he felt he needed to get a good, close look so he wouldn't miss a thing, and her elbow would just have to deal with grazing his body.

She wished she were across the room, or even better, in another state! "Uh, did you make such a close inspection when your other nanny did this?"

"I was busy with work. You're my teacher, Quinn."

This was a break. At least he wouldn't be able to tell when she fouled up royally. She prayed she had enough innate intelligence and maternal instinct so she wouldn't harm the child in her fumbling efforts.

She grasped the baby by one foot and lifted, but that didn't work very well. Tina tipped funny. Still, with this lopsided glimpse, Lauren knew she had a mess on her hands. Trying to hide a grimace, she made a quick survey of the tabletop and spotted some Tot-Mops. She plucked one from its pop-up box. Swallowing hard, she began to clean Tina's tainted little backside. She worked carefully and slowly, grimly determined. When she'd seen these little damp squares of tissue used on TV, it hadn't taken seven of them to do the job! Luckily a covered wastebasket sat nearby. She could open it with her foot, so she quickly disposed of the yucky things.

"A diaper, please?" she said through gritted teeth. The last thing she wanted was a *cloth* diaper.

He held one out.

"Just—put it down."

When he obliged, she closed her eyes and counted to ten. *Let me be able to do this!* She released Tina to squirm on the plastic surface and eyed the diaper with hostility. The dreaded thing was more oblong than square. That was a stupid shape for a diaper! A *shawl,* maybe.

She sucked in a breath, then blew it out. It was now or never! She made a snap decision and folded it, creating a triangle—more or less. Mainly less. Not happy with the weird shape, she made another fold. This time, it was no less weird, but smaller. It *might* work, though it looked like it had been in a head-on collision with a bigger, stronger triangle.

Holding onto her bravado, she raised both of Tina's legs in one hand and scooted the diaper under her. Quickly she lifted the middle point up between Tina's legs and folded the other points around her middle to meet the anchoring point. There was a fairly huge overlap. A pessimistic person might even say the thing was a complete failure. However, not having the luxury of pessimism, Lauren boldly retrieved the fasteners from the place she'd pinned them on her sleeve, and affixed the ends in place. Tina's diaper looked like it had wings.

"That's interesting," Mr. Delacourte murmured. "I don't remember seeing her in anything like that before."

Lauren's bluster was a painfully thin subterfuge, but she had no choice but to forge on. "It's a new fold."

"What's it called, the Boeing 747?"

Her lips twitched with wayward humor, but she refused to allow him to see. Instead she concentrated on getting Tina into her plastic pants and romper. "Where shall I put the soiled diaper, sir?"

"There's a pail in the bathroom, on your right."

She peered in that direction and nodded, then presented him with his daughter. "Please hold her for a moment, while I dispose of it and wash my hands."

His expression was priceless, though irritating. He seemed as startled by being offered his child as he might be if she'd asked him to hold her spleen. "Haven't you ever held her?"

He frowned slightly. "Not—often. I've been busy."

He'd been busy! All the time and money she'd spent these past six months trying to find Tina, longing to be near Tina, and he'd been busy! She imploded with rage and suffering so acute she could hardly contain herself. This man had housed, fed and clothed her precious niece for nearly half a year, but he had scarcely *held* her? Lauren redoubled her vow to get the child out of his indifferent clutches. The selfish playboy was merely warehousing her, not raising her!

Maintaining her poised masquerade was nearly impossible, but she struggled to appear professional. She handed the child to him as gently as her mood would allow. "I don't understand why you want to learn to diaper her, when you—"

"As I said before, Miss Quinn," he cut in, "it's not your place to understand *why* I choose to do anything. Is that clear?"

"Crystal clear, sir," she murmured, stiffly.

He was the master and she the servant. Period. If the great and powerful Dade Delacourte had an urge to learn to diaper Tina, the reason was *not* Lauren's business. She had a sinking feeling that, whatever the reason, the urge would be fleeting—just like any culpability he might feel. Ultimately Tina would be relegated to the care of a series of nannies and nurses, while receiving a very unsavory moral education.

The innocent baby had to be rescued—*and quickly.*

Dade left the nanny and her charge to their privacy and went upstairs to unpack. Alone in his room, he berated himself for snapping at the woman. It wasn't her fault he'd been saddled with a child his brother fathered. It wasn't Quinn's fault Dade felt like a damned failure.

Dade caught sight of himself in a wall mirror and his gut clenched. For a moment he stared at the grim facade, then lurched away. The vision held too much pain. Even his own reflection reminded him of his identical twin, and how badly Dade had unknowingly neglected him.

It didn't seem like eleven years since he'd taken over his father's small electronics firm, welcoming its challenges and opportunities. Unlike himself, Dade's identical twin, Joel, never found his niche in the world. So Dade had sustained his brother's wanderlust lifestyle, mopping up after him when he screwed up. In retrospect, all the paid fines and advances in allowances seemed more like a betrayal to his brother than real assistance.

So now, at his leisure, Dade was free to suffer great guilt. He spent his days and nights eaten up with regret for plunging all his efforts and passions into building the company, rather than taking more personal care to curb his brother's heedless behavior.

His masculine retreat of weathered wood, earth tones and simple furnishings held no peace for him. The wide-plank flooring was so solidly built, it made no revealing sounds as he paced.

"I should have made you come home, take a job with the firm," Dade muttered, jerking a hand through his hair. "I should have *made* you be responsible for your actions."

How could he have let his only family slip so negligently through his fingers? And how quickly, ruthlessly, it was done. On a rainy country road, Joel barreled drunkenly off a cliff to meet a fiery end. Such a tragic waste.

"I'm sorry, Joel." Dade dropped wearily into a leather armchair. "I'm so sorry."

In an ironic twist, Dade didn't actually lose his entire family that night. Though he wouldn't know it until half a year later—when Joel's daughter was born.

He pictured the baby, napping downstairs, and frowned. The last thing Dade wanted was the responsibility of another man's child, yet he couldn't abandon little Christina. Taking her in was one more "fix" of Joel's lamentable life, a huge one—*a last one*—but ultimately, Dade's burden to bear.

His brother was gone, and it was obvious the striking blonde, in the hospital photograph, had no interest in the child. He had heard nothing from her. No demands for money or position. Over the past few months it had become clear that the woman had wanted nothing but to be rid of the child. To that end, she had schemed and plotted, devising exactly how best to force Dade into accountability, since he was the man she *thought* to be the father of her child.

Though she was wrong about his paternity, she was *not* wrong about his obligation.

His grief for all that had been lost was as bitter as his fury at himself. He had forfeited his self-absorbed independence with the shocking arrival of his brother's child. Yet, it was no one's fault but his own.

"I failed you, brother," he muttered. His knuckles whitened as he clutched the chair arms. "In the name of all that's holy, I will *not* fail your daughter."

CHAPTER THREE

LAUREN was out of her element when it came to taking care of an infant. Fortunately Braga, the cook, had received the baby's food menu and schedule early, and the baby's formula was ready when Tina woke from her nap. The menu included "solid" food, so when Braga asked which "solid food" did Nanny prefer, Lauren had a momentary panic attack, and blurted that she was of the school of thought that a baby should have only a bottle at midafternoon.

Braga, a rotund, bulldog of a woman in her mid-fifties, didn't even blink at Lauren's stiff-lipped pronouncement, and indifferently handed over the warmed bottle. With a tiny sigh, Lauren thanked providence for the small reprieve. Her Solid Food Ordeal would be put off until sometime tonight. Right now, her main problem was mastering The Bottle.

She decided to take her niece out onto the acres of redwood deck that surrounded the ocean side of the house. Not necessarily because the day was balmy, but because she thought she would have more privacy to make any blunders in feeding a baby.

The sun shone pleasantly, not overly warm, but Lauren decided a tiny person's skin might be pretty sensitive, so she settled with Tina in a shaded, cushioned lounge chair. To Lauren's surprise and pleasure, the chair rocked.

She managed to get Tina to take the bottle without much problem. Luckily Tina seemed to be a good eater. Relieved, Lauren breathed deeply of the ocean-scented air. How pleasant it was there, with a picture-book view and gentle breeze. The only sounds were the distant sough of the ocean, and the cry of gulls as they swooped and soared.

In such vast, idyllic privacy, Lauren decided to try out a lullaby. After all, she was a music appreciation teacher. She should know lullabies. She began to sing and rock as Tina contentedly took her bottle. After Lauren sang the only verse she knew of "Rock-a-bye Baby" twelve times, she began to get a little sick of it. Besides, who in her right mind would rock a baby in a treetop!

She began to hum one of her favorite compositions by Debussy. Lauren had never considered herself much of a singer, but she could carry a tune. She figured at just under six months of age Tina wouldn't be too picky.

The baby appeared fascinated by Lauren's face and the sound of her voice. Lauren grinned. Something about the sight of those big blue eyes, so wide and rapt, sparked a creative bent in her soul, and she started ad-libbing lyrics. "Oh— Oh, no—not a tree! We don't want to be hauled up in a tree! We're tired of falling—out of *treeeeeeees.*"

"I didn't realize Clair de lune had words."

Lauren jerked around to see Mr. Delacourte framed in the open door to the living room. He'd changed into blue shorts, deck shoes and a white polo shirt. He was marvelous looking, breathtakingly so, from a great pair of legs to his masterfully chiseled face. A smile lurked in dazzling smoky-gray eyes. Once again he was laughing at her.

She hid her embarrassment at being caught spouting such an inane song, and returned her gaze to Tina. She was surprised that he recognized Clair de lune. But since it was a sensual melody, she supposed he'd used it for a few seductions in his time. "I—I made up the words."

"Really?" The smile spread to his voice. "Sounds like some of my college roommate's stuff."

"Thank you." She had a feeling his remark wasn't a wholehearted compliment, but she didn't intend to let him know. "Your roommate was a musical genius, I gather."

He grinned. "My roommate thought so."

She peered his way, telling herself his dimpled smile had no effect on her. "Actually there's a school of thought—that babies should hear the classics early and often." She didn't know if there was such a school, but if there wasn't, there should be.

She stroked Tina's downy hair as the baby sucked out the last of her formula. Lifting the empty bottle away, Lauren placed it on a small, glass-topped table beside her chair. "Tina's encouraging expression got the better of me," she added honestly. "I felt the urge to combat any negative suggestions that she allow herself to be—"

"Dropped from a tree?"

Lauren eyed him again, exasperated by his obvious mirth. "Well, if you ask me, it's a stupid lullaby."

"It always seemed stupid to me." He moved to the railing and gazed out to sea. Lauren's glance trailed over him. Being a pragmatic woman, she told herself Dade Delacourte looked *exactly* like any other man in his mid-thirties. Well, perhaps any other really good-looking man in his mid-thirties.

His dark hair fluttered in the breeze, shiny-clean

and soft. It was only hair, she reminded herself. And he was *only* a man, like billions of others. *Broader around the shoulders, squarer of jaw and appealingly tall,* a wayward imp in her brain taunted. *With to-die-for legs and drool-worthy dimples. Not to mention, he's richer than practically any man in the country!* She shook her head to squelch the disturbing imp.

Mr. Delacourte didn't *look* like a heartless womanizer. Maybe that was the problem with heartless womanizers. They didn't wear warning signs, and their claws didn't show. All one actually saw was the pleasant manly trappings.

Much later than she should have, Lauren tugged her attention away from his broad back. It was a shame she couldn't see his claws, even sadder that there were no outward signs of his negligent heart.

How unfair!

Lauren frowned as she lifted Tina to her shoulder and began to pat. She knew this was how one burped a baby. A person couldn't make it into her mid-twenties without at least seeing a baby being burped. "Okay, Tina. Do it for Aun—" She cut herself off. *How could she have started to say Auntie Lauren, with Dade Delacourte right there! Was she going noodley in the head?* She coughed to cover her mistake. "...for Quinn."

She patted and patted. After a minute, a very unladylike trumpet bellowed out of the infant. The deep belch took Lauren so by surprise, she burst out laughing.

Dade turned, looking puzzled. "What's funny?"

Lauren pursed her lips and shook her head. No nanny worth her salt would laugh at a burp, no matter how much it sounded like an off-key toot of a French horn. "Nothing." She swallowed a giggle, making sure her features registered businesslike reserve. "Her burp—is quite—musical."

"Is that what you'd call it?" He flashed a grin and her pulse grew fitful. He shifted around to face her, and leaned against the rail. "Are you saying she has talent, Miss Quinn?"

"I'd give that burp an A-plus—for volume, anyway." Lauren batted down an urge to smile at him, reminding herself why she was here and exactly who and what this man was. "Does she get her burping talent from you?"

His amusement vanished. For an instant his gaze rested on the child, his features vaguely troubled; then he turned away.

His reaction startled Lauren. "Uh, I didn't mean to offend you." Good grief, didn't the man have a sense of humor? Apparently he could laugh at her, but woe be it to anybody who dared joke about him!

"Did you find everything satisfactory in your rooms, Quinn?" he asked, his voice low and controlled.

She absently patted Tina's back, watching him. Evidently there were rules about nanniness she needed to commit to memory. Like, "Don't kid with your employer." Well, that was *fine* with her. The less casual chatting between them, the better. "The rooms are fine, sir."

"Good." He didn't turn.

Beeeerrrrrttthhhh!

Tina's second showy belch made Lauren jump. She experienced another titter of laughter, but hid it under a manufactured coughing fit. She repositioned Tina into the crook of her arm, smiled at the baby and began to rock. "Where did you learn your manners, sweetie?" she whispered.

Something flitted into Lauren's peripheral vision. Even before she registered what she saw, her adrenaline surged. She snapped her gaze up to fasten on the flitting thing. *A wasp!* Her sister, Millie, was terribly allergic to wasp stings, and at four-years-old had almost died from a sting. What if Tina had inherited the same allergic reaction?

The wasp swooped too near the baby. Lauren bent forward to protect Tina with her body. *"No!"* She swatted at the insect. "Get out of here you *devil!*"

"Excuse me?"

Lauren didn't have the time to concern herself with Mr. Delacourte's sensibilities. Let him think she'd called him a devil. It wasn't as though the thought had never crossed her mind. She crouched over Tina, peeking around to see where the wasp was. She whacked at it, but missed again. *"Get away!"*

The winged pest dived out of her range of vision, but a second later she knew where it went from the stinging at her nape. *"Ouch!"*

"Damn!"

Lauren hardly had time to register the growled curse. She found herself relieved of the baby and tugged from the chair. A large hand gripped her upper arm. "Are you allergic, Quinn?"

"No—not particularly—it just stings." Once she had her bearings, she realized Dade held the baby against his chest with one arm and hauled her with the other. "I'll be okay," she said. "Just make sure Tina's safe."

"That wasp won't bother anybody now."

Once inside, Dade led Lauren to the kitchen and

coaxed her to sit at the breakfast table. "Take the baby." He handed Tina back and strode toward a cabinet.

Lauren winced at the stinging in her neck, but regained enough of her wits to glance around. Besides Dade, the baby and her, the kitchen was empty. Yet the place was redolent with the rich scent of roasting beef. Tentatively she touched the smarting bump, and winced. "Where's the cook?" she asked.

"Shopping for tomorrow's meals." Dade retrieved a box of baking soda from a cabinet and poured some into a cup, then added a little water.

"What's that?"

"It should take the sting out."

She stared. "You know a remedy for wasp stings?" She wouldn't have thought he was the type to know such homespun tidbits. She figured a man like Dade Delacourte would be more likely to know the gross national product of Uruguay rather than a balm for insect stings.

"I spent summers on my grandparents' farm in Vermont." He glanced her way, his brows knit. "When they died, they left the place to me. I moved the barn here and turned it into my house." He dropped the spoon into the sink and returned to her.

"Really?" Lauren murmured. Sentiment? She supposed even womanizers could have fond memories of grandparents. But this sentimental side of him surprised her. If that's what it was. Maybe his reasons were purely narcissistic or, just as likely, some kind of tax write-off. Who knew? "It's—very nice," she said, meaning it. No matter why he'd moved the barn all this way to create his rustic haven, it had turned out wonderfully.

"Thanks." He scooped some of the white goo onto his fingertips. "Lean forward."

With great reluctance, she did as he commanded. Though she wasn't as allergic to wasp stings as Millie, they stung like crazy and made a good-size welt.

Earlier that afternoon, while Tina napped, Lauren had swept her hair up off her neck with a big clip. Now she regretted the action for two reasons. First, it had made it easier for a wasp to sting her neck, which brought on the second, and most troubling regret—Dade Delacourte's fingers gently brushed sensitive skin as he smoothed warm paste on the wound.

Dade's touch sent shivers of appreciation along Lauren's spine. She supposed playboys had to cultivate a seductive touch or they wouldn't be successful at—playing. She recognized the sad irony, but wasn't in the mood for ironic life lessons at the moment. She chewed her lower lip, her emotions in conflict. She wanted his hand *off* her, but a niggling part of her brain wouldn't allow her to jerk away.

"I'm sorry about the touching, Quinn." He sounded as though he was only half teasing. "Unfortunately salve goes on better with fingers than a butter knife."

She grimaced at his light taunt. Gathering her antagonism around her like a protective cloak, she cleared her throat loudly. "I understand the necessity, Mr. Delacourte, though I find it *quite* off-putting."

Her remark bordered on rudeness, and she sounded like a Victorian spinster, but she was upset, and it just came out that way. Why did she have to find his touch so *far* from off-putting? Hadn't Millie's fate taught her anything about this man?

On the other hand, Mr. Delacourte didn't have to help her. She owed him a debt for doctoring her. "Nonetheless, I would be remiss if I didn't say thank you for..." His free hand stroked her neck and she caught her breath. *"What do you think you're doing!"*

"Moving loose strands out of the way." He sounded slightly annoyed. "Don't be so paranoid."

Her resentment billowed. She couldn't make a tiny joke about him, but he felt no compunction about insulting her! "I'm not paranoid!" she retorted. "Your reputation with women isn't exactly a secret!"

"My rep...what reputation?"

She eyed him mistrustfully. "*What reputation?* Are you suggesting you *ordered* your daughter from a catalog?"

His jawline hardened, and angry color spread beneath the tan of his face. "How clever of you to be so perfect, Quinn." His lips curled cynically. "You must feel quite superior to the rest of us." His eyes sparked with resentment. The cup he held thudded to the tabletop a heartbeat before he turned and strode away.

A stab of self-reproach made her cringe. For somebody *supposedly* so "clever," that crack about the catalog was a real gem. "Start packing, Lauren, old girl," she muttered. "If anybody ever deserved to be fired, you do."

How could she have acted like such a nincompoop? Maybe part of it could be blamed on the fact that she hadn't slept since yesterday, and she'd eaten nothing all day but a handful of airline peanuts. Even so, that was no excuse for lashing out at him—however legitimate the charge. She needed to remember that Mr.

Delacourte was not only a powerful adversary, he was her *boss!*

At least for a few more minutes.

She glanced at Tina; her precious niece smiled and cooed, the image of the angel she was. Misery flooded Lauren. What if Mr. Delacourte *did* fire her? When would she see Tina again?

Maybe never!

Fear pierced her heart like white-hot shards of metal, and she cast a pleading glance toward heaven. Nobody knew better than she, all that would be lost if Mr. Delacourte booted her out. "I won't shoot off my mouth, again!" she whispered brokenly. "*Please* give me another chance!"

Lauren hustled Tina to the privacy of their rooms. She found a baby quilt in one of Tina's dresser drawers, and spread it out in front of the patio doors in her room. She did the best she could to forget that any minute Goodberry would arrive to help pack her bag and return her to Manhattan. At least she hoped Mr. Delacourte would do more than just set her out on the highway to thumb her way back.

No matter how many times she jumped at sounds outside the door, nobody burst in shouting, "You're fired," and flinging her walking papers in her face. Nobody even knocked. She and Tina simply lay on the blanket, Lauren delighting in Tina's enjoyment of the noises of her squeeze toys. After a while, they merely exchanged baby jabber and smiles. Except for the "You're fired" burden hanging over Lauren's head, she couldn't recall spending a more pleasant afternoon in her life.

She changed Tina's diaper, without noticeable improvement. This one looked less like a jetliner and more like a rabbit with one big, droopy ear and one stunted one. Luckily, since Mr. Delacourte wasn't there to witness the latest defective attempt, she tucked the floppy "ear" inside the waist and slipped the plastic pants on. Plastic pants were a wonderful invention, she decided. Besides keeping the world a little dryer, they hid a multitude of diapering faux pas.

Tina lay on her stomach, arching up and kicking her feet, happily gurgling and drooling. After a rousing game of Throw The Rattle, the infant grew droopy eyed, and lay her head on the blanket, content to smile and coo at Lauren.

In order to give the child easier access to her face, Lauren rested her cheek on the blanket. They gibber-jabbered back and forth, watching each other, their faces at close proximity. After a while Tina's eyes closed. Lauren smiled at her sleeping niece. Tina had fine, curly blond hair, like Millie's. And she had Millie's heart-shaped mouth and her ears. But not Millie's eyes. Tina had long, curling lashes, and though her eyes were still baby-blue, Lauren sensed they would one day be the striking pearl-gray of her father's.

Whatever else might have been rash and wrong with the brief liaison between Millie and Mr. Delacourte, Lauren knew Tina was not a part of it. She was beautiful, sweet and precious. Lauren's heart filled with a love so powerful, it could hardly have been more maternal if she'd borne the child herself.

The sun had traveled too far west to shine in the room, but its warmth lingered. Tina smelled of talcum and the pure essence of baby. A nice combination. Everything was very still.

Drained, physically and emotionally, Lauren's limbs felt like lead, her mind like wet gauze. She had endured months of worry, the stress of the desperate flight to a place she'd never been and was far from welcome. Then, suddenly, here she was, thrust into this bizarre deception—playacting a part she was unqualified for. To top it off, she was now *living with* her nemesis. She couldn't recall a time when she'd been this mentally exhausted. Not meaning to—fighting it with all her might—her eyelids drooped, and fluttered shut.

"Quinn!"

Lauren's head jerked up. As her muscles recoiled, she banged her chin. She cringed at the pain and peered, disgruntled, at a pair of dock shoes planted not far away. Groggy, she came up on an elbow, squinting up, up, up, into Mr. Delacourte's face. Her chin hurt. She wondered if there was a salve for what ailed her? "Sir?" She grimaced at the dopey way it came out.

"Were you asleep?" he asked in a gruff whisper.

"No—sir." She tried to stifle a yawn. *Heavenly days!* Had she fallen asleep? She must have, or surely she would have noticed a huge man like Mr. Delacourte coming up to tower above her. "I—I mean..."

What excuse did she have? What excuse was there? She'd fallen asleep on duty! She'd shouted at her boss not long ago, and now she was sleeping on duty. If she'd been in the army, she would be standing, blindfolded, in front of a firing squad.

She cast a fearful glance at Tina. Her niece slept

on, just the way Lauren last saw her, before she'd been so derelict in her duty and dozed off. "I'm—I'm sorry!" She took a deep breath, to get a quick blast of oxygen to her groggy brain.

Get a grip, Lauren! she charged inwardly. *You already had one foot out the door. Are you going to hand him the ammunition to launch you the rest of the way out?* "Uh, er, I mean, I'm so sorry I didn't notice you, sir. You see..." She thought fast. "You...see...according to—" her gaze darted around for any word to latch onto and the wicker settee sprang into her line of vision "—to Wicker-burg, er, *Dr.* Wickerburger—in his research of the, uh, Child Growth Trust Continuum..."

She cleared her throat. She was out of fancy words, and shook her head to stall. "It's complicated." She shrugged, hoping the move would convey that he, the average-layman-non-child-care-professional, would never grasp even a simplified version of what she was doing. "Be assured Dr. Wickerstein is world-renowned, and his theories well-founded." That was a big, fat lie, but considering the fact that her name wasn't Quinn and she was no more a nanny than she was a jet pilot, this lie was small change.

"I thought it was Wickerburger."

She experienced a prick of annoyance at herself for the mistake—and at him for his infuriatingly sharp memory. "Er, it is. Dr. Wickle Wickerburger."

"Wickle?" He sounded incredulous. "Wickle Wickerburger is this baby guru's name?"

Wickle! She couldn't blame him for his skepticism. What would have been so wrong about making up a name like John? Not a thing! But, no, she had to blurt out *Wickle!* She supposed she was so hungry her subconscious veered toward burgers and Wickles, er pickles. She fought an impulse to kick herself. "There's no need to make fun of his name, sir. Dr. Wickerburger wouldn't make fun of yours."

His laughter rumbled low. "With a name like Wickle Wickerburger, that would be wise."

Lauren pushed back an urge to grin at his dry wit, and responded sternly, "No matter what you think of his name, Dr. Wickerburger applauds the technique I was using."

Her boss squatted, his expression dubious. They were nearer eye-to-eye, though he still loomed ominously. "When the doctor's applause dies down, Quinn, dinner's ready."

"Oh..." Lauren was so thankful for that news she wanted to cry. "Actually," she improvised, "once the baby has fallen into a Growth Trust Sleep—which she has—the exercise is terminated for the day." Rising to her knees, she swept a stray wisp of hair out of her face. "I'll slip her into bed and be right out."

He stood, eyed her for a long moment, then extended a hand, indicating her face. "You've got a little Growth Trust Sleep pattern on your cheek, Miss Quinn." His grin was sardonic. "Do we still hear Dr. Wickerbasket applauding?"

"Wickerchair!" She flinched. "I mean—*burger!*" Now she not only had the pattern of the blanket on her cheek, but she was as purple as a turnip for her embarrassing slip. "I'll only be a minute."

"See that you are," he said quietly, in deference to his sleeping daughter. "We have work to do."

She'd scooped up her limp, dozing charge, but her head went up. "We—we do?"

"You're my teacher, remember?" He angled toward the door, glancing back. "I expect you to teach."

When he was gone, Lauren clutched the baby to her breast and squeezed her eyes shut. "Oh, Tina," she moaned, feeling sick to her stomach. "And I used to think directing the fifth-grade boys a cappella chorus was my worst nightmare." She came sluggishly to her feet and trudged to the crib. "What a blissfully naive fool I was!"

Dade felt like a jerk. He hadn't given a thought to Miss Quinn since she'd arrived. At least not a thought about her problems. She'd been over an hour late, but had he bothered to ask why? It was obvious she was exhausted, for whatever reason. No wonder she'd snapped at him earlier. If she could fall into such a sound sleep that he had to practically shout at her to wake her, she was dead on her feet.

With the baby sleeping right there, he hadn't actually shouted, but he'd called her name four times before she stirred—and bopped herself on the chin. His lips twitched. She wouldn't even allow herself a yelp of pain. He had to give her credit. She was very professional, this one. Maybe a little puritanical and tightly wound—and that stilted vocabulary! He wondered if she ever cried out, *"Oh, baby!"* in the throes of lovemaking. She probably shouted, "Quite a good job!"

He frowned at the sexual turn of mind. Where in blazes did that come from? The last thing on earth he intended to do was breach any teacher-pupil or employee-employer relationship between them. Puritanical and tightly wound though she was, Miss Quinn loved children. That was clear. Her expression changed when she looked at Tina. She was softer, her cheeks pinker, her eyes sparkled. The change in her was fascinating to watch.

His first nanny had been competent, but she didn't love Tina. Quinn clearly did. Observing such depth of devotion in Quinn's behavior, Dade decided he could put up with her snappishness and snobbishness. Nobody was perfect, and he could certainly endure her barbed personality for Tina's sake. It was the child's well-being he had to concern himself with. And Quinn would be good to Tina.

He stood beside the long pine table, waiting for Quinn. When she peeked around the corner, looking sheepish and a little lost, he beckoned. "We haven't moved the dining room since you arrived, Quinn. It's still here."

She stepped inside the double-doored entry. "But—Braga must be wrong. She said I was to eat in here."

He pulled out a chair. "You are."

"But—with you?"

He nodded toward the chair. "I said we have work to do, Quinn. I didn't think discussing child care in the dining room, over pot roast, would be a breach of etiquette."

She swallowed, and his lips quirked with amusement. "Why are you acting like a mouse? Where did your last employer make you take meals, on the back porch with stray cats?"

She shook her head, and seemed to gather courage. "Of course not." She walked in, but she looked uncomfortable. "I just—usually eat in the kitchen."

"Not here." He picked up a thick volume that lay beside his place at the head of the table. "I bought ten books on child care, but for some reason this is the only one that made it out here. The others are doubtless sitting in a box in my office.'' He held the paperback up for her to see. ''It's not by Dr. Wicker-whatever, but somebody named Dr. Duane Applebee. I hope you approve.''

She stared at the book as she made her way around the table. Standing very still, she perused the paper-back's cover until Dade thought she'd slipped into another of her trances. ''Miss Quinn?''

She jumped and peered at him. ''Yes?''

''Do you approve of the book?''

Shc nodded somewhat disjointedly. ''I—I'm not familiar with his...theories.'' She lifted the book from his fingers. ''Perhaps it would be better if I scanned it tonight, then we can discuss it tomorrow.''

''I prefer to start tonight. I've read the first several chapters, and I have a few questions.'' He held her chair. ''Please join me.''

She looked at him, appearing confused. He indi-cated the chair with a nod. ''Sit?''

''Oh...'' She fell heavily into the chair. ''What... exactly would you care to discuss...tonight?''

He took the book from her fingers, though it wasn't easy. ''I thought we'd start at the beginning.'' He seated himself. As he adjusted his chair, his leg brushed hers, and she immediately moved away. He glanced her way, puzzled. Besides being tightly wound and puritanical, she was as skittish as a colt. He supposed, for whatever reason, she was simply more comfortable with children than adults. Or pos-sibly she was afraid of men.

He glanced at her in time to see her avert her gaze.

Whether it was men, plural, or man, singular, she seemed to dislike him. There was no reason to. True, he'd been a bit gruff when they'd first met, but he wasn't an ogre. He'd never had trouble keeping employees.

He frowned in thought. Had some man hurt her? Of course her past wasn't his affair. Quinn was an employee with knowledge he needed. Period. He didn't intend to burden her with his troubles, so the best thing would be to allow her to deal with hers in her own way.

"What is the first chapter about?" she asked, drawing him back.

Braga came in with the steaming platter of pot roast and its accompanying potatoes and carrots. While Dade sliced meat and served them both, Braga poured coffee, then left them to their privacy.

"The first chapter," Dade said, flipping the pages. "'Your Baby Won't Break.'" He glanced at her with a wry twist of his lips. "Apparently our doctor Duane has no qualms about cradles falling from treetops."

His nanny darted him a startled look. A heartbeat later, amusement flickered in her eyes, and she smiled.

Dade's response was intensely physical and he found himself momentarily speechless. Who would have guessed that his puritanical, tightly wound little nanny could turn a simple smile into a sensual experience?

CHAPTER FOUR

LAUREN realized she was smiling at her boss like some kind of Sappy-Sally-Smilie doll. So what if he was vaguely amusing from time to time. Men like him honed their wit to a razor's edge, for the precise purpose of slicing away at a woman's resistance.

She squelched her grin and returned her attention to her dinner. First, and foremost, she had to eat or she would be of no good to herself or Tina. Passing out from starvation wouldn't get the goods on Mr. Delacourte's wild, wanton womanizing.

She stabbed a piece of roast beef, so tender it fell away from the rest of the slice like loosely packed snow. She took a bite, and couldn't help but close her eyes, savoring the exquisite taste. She supposed it could have tasted like chalk, and it wouldn't matter. She was so hungry. But the flavor didn't bear any resemblance to chalk. Braga may be an unsmiling, gruff woman, but she could cook for the gods on Olympus.

"Quinn?"

Lauren heard him, and snapped to glance his way. He watched her quizzically, as though he was afraid she'd lapsed into some kind of bizarre coma in which the victim could do nothing but chew. "Yes, Mr. Delacourte?"

"Call me Dade." He grinned, the conniving *rat.*

"Oh, I don't think that would be—"

"Look, Quinn. I'll call you whatever you want.

Quinn, Miss Quinn or Hey You, if that's what you prefer. But since you and I will be spending so much time together, and you'll be acting as my teacher, I insist you call me Dade."

Against her will she stared into his eyes. They narrowed as she watched. He didn't appear flexible on the subject. "Shall we continue?"

Fierce objections clamored at her lips, but the flare of his nostrils made her see that he would have none of her rigid dictates. She decided calling him Dade didn't compromise her mission or her morals, so she nodded. "Certainly. If you insist, sir."

"Dade."

"Of course—Dade."

"Thank you, Quinn."

She imagined he expected her to offer a first name, now. Unfortunately she couldn't. He knew more about the real Quinn than she did. Even if she wanted to, she couldn't because she didn't know what it was. She turned her attention to her meal. "You're welcome." She took another bite of beef.

He cleared his throat. "Chapter One is relatively self-explanatory. I have only a few questions." She heard a clink as he lay his fork aside, and glanced in his direction in time to see him refer to The Book. She experienced a shiver of trepidation. Temporarily her need for food had allowed her to forget The Book. Heavens! She wasn't up to a test on child care! She was hardly up to staying awake. Since he'd actually *read* Chapter One, he was already way ahead of her! "It states here—"

"Excuse me, sir."

Lauren recognized Goodberry's voice and experienced a swell of relief for the interruption. He stood in the kitchen doorway. A slight frown wrinkled his brow.

"Yes, Goodberry?" Mr. Delacourte said.

"The child is crying."

Lauren blinked, startled. She glanced down at her belt, where she'd fastened the baby monitor. "I don't understand. Nothing's registering."

Mr. Delacourte's hand came into her view, and he touched the little device. "Perhaps turning it on would help."

The minute he flipped the switch, Lauren could hear Tina's shrill yells. "Oh—dear." Lauren's face burned. "I—" She faced her boss and worked on keeping poised as she made a weak excuse. "In the dark room—well, this isn't exactly like the one I had..."

Mr. Delacourte waved off her explanation. "No harm done. You'd better go check on her, though. Hadn't you?"

She was halfway out of the dining room before he finished speaking. "She's probably hungry." Actually Lauren had no idea what might be wrong, and she prayed the diaper pins weren't poking her. Something that horrible could only be due to her ineptitude! She couldn't stand the idea of hurting her precious niece. "Goodberry," she called as she rushed past, "have Braga prepare some solid food."

Lauren hoped Braga had instructions on how to do that, because she had no idea.

"Any particular menu, miss?" Goodberry asked.

"No—" She slowed, turned. "There's—a—a school of thought that states—variety stimulates the brain." She spun away, berating herself for being such an ignoramus on the subject of babies. Still, she didn't think feeding Tina green beans and bananas at eight o'clock at night rather than meat and potatoes could scar the child's psyche very badly.

After Lauren checked her niece for offending pins and discovered she was not only free from any stab wounds but was also dry, she breathed a sigh. She carried the baby to the kitchen in time to see Goodberry retrieve a high chair from the pantry. Lauren was a little concerned, since she hadn't seen Tina do much *erect* sitting. Then she noticed the seat belt. Pretending she buckled babies into high chairs every day, she gently lowered Tina into the narrow space between the seat back and tray.

"Wouldn't it be easier to lift up the tray?"

Lauren flicked a gaze at Dade as he came in from the dining room. She didn't respond as she settled Tina in the chair. *Yes,* she thought grudgingly, *it would have been much easier, if I had had any idea the tray lifted up!* Buckling her niece was difficult, because her hands shook. Why couldn't Dade stay away! Goodberry and Braga didn't unsettle her the way her boss did. Of course, the way he scrutinized her every move so closely, was enough to drive a *real* nanny nuts. Or maybe her agitation was simply due to the fact that she so abhorred the man, everything he did disturbed her.

"Here's her dinner, Miss Quinn."

Lauren accepted a deep, segmented ceramic plate from Braga. With a murmured thank-you, she eyed the stuff in the dish. One pile of glop was brownish, one was greenish and the third, orangish. It looked like organic finger paint.

"What did you prepare?" she asked, hoping the question didn't brand her as a rank amateur.

"Beef, peas and sweet potatoes. I didn't know if you'd want her to have any fruit or pudding this late."

Lauren had no idea, either, but shook her head. "This is fine for tonight."

"The schedule mentions a bottle of formula, but since you fed her one this afternoon, I didn't know if I should heat up another."

Lauren cleared her throat. She didn't have the vaguest idea, so she improvised. "Warm it, and I'll take it into her room with me and give it to her before I put her back to bed."

"Yes, miss."

Lauren felt a tiny bit calmer at that relatively painless save. She glanced at Tina, who whimpered and slapped the tray with the flats of both tiny hands. Clearly the infant was ready for food. Lauren knew exactly how she felt. Three bites of roast beef hadn't exactly satisfied her hunger pangs.

Lauren glanced at the dish in her hand. She didn't know how to put it on the tray with Tina banging away, so she opted to hold it. She sat down in a nearby chair. "Okay, Tina, honey. Food's coming." She glanced at the dish and hesitated. How was Tina supposed to eat it? She started to get up to go find some utensils, but was almost smashed in the nose by a tiny silver spoon.

Dade held it out in long masculine fingers, making the sterling piece of flatware seem like a fugitive from a dollhouse. "You might need this," he said.

Without looking into his face, she took it. "Yes, I was just about to get that." She mumbled a diffident thank-you and turned to her fussy charge. Now the biggest problem was, did Tina hold the spoon and eat her own dinner, or did Lauren feed it to her? *Rats,* she wished everybody would go away and leave them alone.

The sound of wood scraping against wood made it clear that her boss was seating himself. No doubt planning to observe her every *professional* move with the close scrutiny of a scientist peering through a microscope at a germ! Oh, why couldn't she have had a chance to scan that book!

She lifted her chin, and made a decision. "Here, Tina." She placed the spoon in the baby's hand. Tina promptly slammed it hard on the tray top. *Whack! Whack! Whack! Whack!* The noise didn't seem to please Tina, because she began to cry. An instant later, the spoon walloped Lauren squarely in the chest.

"Oh!" She clamped her lips shut, but not quickly enough to hide her shock. How unprofessional!

"That was interesting," her boss said. "What was the point?"

She fished the spoon from her lap and made herself look at him. "I—you see, there's a school of thought—that states, 'Give the child choices and—and challenges.'" Lauren paused, her brain staggering around for any straw to grasp. "Tina, er, has informed me that she is not yet prepared to feed herself."

"I gather that's another of Dr. Wickerburger's theories?"

Lauren nodded, removing her gaze from his, which was too skeptical for her frame of mind. She dipped the baby spoon into the brownish glop.

"According to Dr. Applebee," he said, "babies can't feed themselves until they're almost a year old."

Drat Dade Delacourte! Why did he have to have The Book! She aimed the brown stuff toward Tina's mouth and prayed for success. "Dr. Wickerburger," she began, with as much authority as she could muster, "and his adherents, are not bound by unprogressive dogma and methodologies, sir." *Please, Tina,* she cried telepathically, *make me look good. Be the angel you are and swallow this disgusting ooze.*

To Lauren's amazement and delight, Tina opened her precious mouth and allowed Lauren to stick the spoon inside. The baby closed her lips over the food, so Lauren pulled out the spoon, scraping the food off on Tina's gums and lips as she did. *Eureka! One successful bite!*

Tina made a gurgling sound and stuck her hand into her mouth, swished it around, then drew out mucky brown fingers. With an excited squeal, she banged her hands on the tray. *Wham! Wham! Wham!* Brown muck spattered everywhere. From the damp plop on her chin, Lauren had a hunch, a major tidbit now clung there like a gooey goatee. Another Wham! and Lauren flinched as wet goo splashed on her eyelid.

Tina's face and romper didn't get off lightly. She looked like she'd been spattered by a tire spinning in mud.

"Oh, Tina—" Lauren abruptly broke off her anguished lament. What would a child-care professional do? *A child-care professional would have remembered to put a bib on the baby, stupid!* she raged inwardly. "That was—excellent."

"It was?" Dade sounded dubious.

She cast him a narrowed look. "She has perfect hand-eye coordination."

"If you mean her hand and *your* eye, I have to agree." He grinned. Her heart did a little fluttery dance at the sight. Fortunately Lauren knew a calculating Lothario hid behind that handsome mask. That knowledge had spawned in her an impenetrable resistance to him. Still, she could see how more impressionable women might fall for his disarming charm.

Irritated by the charisma of his grin as well as his everlasting amusement at her expense, she scooped up a spoonful of the orange stuff. Maybe Tina would like it better. "We must never find fault with the child's exploration of tactile stimuli." *What a load of bull!* Lauren didn't know how she thought she was going to pull off this masquerade. She had been an abject failure from the word go, and this humiliating experience was only adding insult to injury. Whoever suggested that the maternal instinct came naturally was a raving lunatic.

She poked the spoonful of sweet potato into Tina's grinning, gurgling mouth and hoped for the best. As she watched, not daring to breathe, Tina pursed her lips around the offering and gummed it. Her hands stayed out of her mouth. Could she possibly be planning to swallow it? Lauren pretended nonchalance and stirred the pasty sweet potatoes as though she had no doubts about a victorious outcome.

"I think she likes the potatoes,' Dade said.

Lauren avoided looking at him, and quickly stuffed in another spoonful. This one, too disappeared with amazing success, but for a hint of orange slobber. Tina took care of it by rubbing her mucky fingers over her mouth and cheeks.

Dade's laugh filled the room, so rich and melodious that even Tina turned his way. She grinned and gurgled, and held out both sticky hands before slamming them on the tray. *Wham! Wham! Wham! Wham!*

Lauren supposed she couldn't blame Tina. Mr. Delacourte had a way about him—that laugh and those devilishly alluring dimples. No doubt females, young and old, reacted with gusto. Lauren's own pulse kept in rapid, thumping tempo with Tina's exuberant whacks.

The next attempt at a bite of sweet potato didn't go as well. Tina spluttered it out and smeared it around her cheeks and in her hair. Lauren kept her poise, and tried the peas. Some went down. Some spurted out like a green geyser. Tina jabbered and drooled and pounded the tray, having a high old time.

Frustrated though she was, Lauren couldn't keep a straight face at the sight. Tina was filthy, but darling. Before Lauren knew it, she was laughing out loud. "You're a sight, sweetie." She shook her head, but when Tina grabbed the bowl of the spoon and scooped out the peas and stuck her hand in her mouth, Lauren couldn't suppress another giggle.

"Should she be allowed to do that?" Dade asked, laughter in his voice.

"If the food gets into her mouth, it's a good thing," Lauren said before she even realized it. Quickly she glanced his way. "There's a school of thought," she amended, "that suggests..." *What! What?*

"If the food gets into her mouth, it's a good thing?" he asked.

"Yes." She flushed and faced Tina. "I'm going to try another technique." She swallowed hard and held a spoonful of beef in the air. "Here comes the train!" She'd seen this on TV. Some sitcom. She hoped the writers knew what they were doing! *"Chug-a-chuga-chug-a-chuga."* She bounced the spoon toward Tina's mouth. *"Chug-a-chuga-chug-a-chuga..."*

Tina seemed quite taken with the undulating spoon, as well as the rhythm of Lauren's voice. With a gleeful, bubbly squeal, she slammed her hands on the tray and opened her mouth. The strained beef went in, was gummed and swallowed. Lauren was so thrilled she almost burst into tears. This baby-feeding thing wasn't so awfully hard! She grinned at her charge and sent another choo-choo train into the choo-choo cave.

Twenty choo-choo trains later, she decided enough of the tricolored goo had been ingested that she could put herself out of her misery, and end the meal. Though she found the time with Tina remarkably enjoyable, she felt like a muck-covered mouse being scrutinized by a very intense hawk, in the form of Dade Delacourte.

From the tainted tips of Tina's golden curls to the entire area of her romper that could be seen above the tray, the infant looked like a finger painting done during a severe earthquake. Lauren didn't look much better. Blotches of baby food dried on her cheek, chin and one eyelid. Several drab blemishes graced the bodice of her shirtwaist.

"She's satisfied." This time Lauren lifted the tray coated with strained food, unfastened Tina and lifted her out of the chair.

"I don't think I'll be ready to try feeding her for a while," Dade said.

Lauren gave him a jaundiced glance. He didn't think he'd be ready to try it for a while? She wanted to shout, "If I can do it, big guy, so can you!" But naturally, she couldn't. His remark merely reinforced her conviction that he would soon lose interest in his daughter, altogether. "No hurry, sir."

"Dade," he corrected.

She lifted her chin, beef goatee and all. "No hurry—Dade." She inhaled, trying to keep her voice level. "There is so much to learn—in order to perfect the technique."

He smiled, displaying those bothersome dimples. "I shudder to think what Tina would look like in the hands of a nonprofessional."

She couldn't decide if he was being sarcastic or sincere, and opted not to respond.

He indicated her room. "Shall we proceed to the bath?"

Lauren's heart dropped. She couldn't deal with any more of his close inspections and interrogations! Not tonight! She needed sleep, and she needed breathing space. "I think you've absorbed enough for one day, Mr., uh, Dade. A bath is very advanced."

His brows dipped slightly, then after a second, he nodded. "Fine. I'll read the rest of Dr. Applebee's book, tonight. We can get back to my hands-on training, tomorrow."

She nodded, the brief stay of execution making her wobbly with relief. "Of course. Good night." She whipped around and gave Braga a sober nod as she passed. Pink-cheeked Goodberry stood by the door. "May I be of help, miss?" He smiled, his expression benevolent.

She decided she liked Goodberry and smiled back. "No, thank you. Tina and I will be fine. Good night."

Panic and nervous stress fueling her exhausted body, she fled.

Once safely inside their private apartment, Lauren

slumped against the door. "I have to get my hands on that book!" she muttered. *"Tonight!"*

Lauren felt like a spy or a burglar, sneaking up the stairs toward Dade's room in the dead of night. She'd already checked the living room and found no sign of The Book, so it had to be in his room. The idea of invading his privacy was unthinkable. But not quite as unthinkable as spending the next vital days, or weeks, gathering proof against him, while floundering around *pretending* to teach him how to care for a child. She couldn't allow Dade to guess the truth. A few more stupid flubs like not knowing the high chair tray lifted up, or forgetting a bib, would surely brand her as a fake.

A step creaked underfoot and she froze. The place was as quiet as outer space, or at least what she figured outer space sounded like. Even though a wall of windows across the open room welcomed in a wide swath of moonlight, the illumination didn't penetrate this far, and it was very dark on the stairs.

Lauren carefully resumed her trek toward Mr. Delacourte's room, her heart hammering. She knew it was the first room to the right of the stairs, for Goodberry had given her a tour earlier. Little did the manservant realize he had been an unknowing accomplice in her crime. Poor sweet man. She only hoped he would never find out. She prayed with all her heart her boss wouldn't. If he caught her she would not only be out on her ear, but probably prosecuted as a Peeping Tom, or worse.

Lauren shook off the thought. She didn't need more stress. She was a nervous wreck as it was—an exhausted nervous wreck. At least she was no longer hungry. Goodberry had brought her a tray right after Tina dropped off to sleep. Lauren felt sure if Goodberry had an inkling of what she intended to do with her revived energy—skulking around like a thief in the night—he would never have fed her. Nevertheless, she *had* to get The Book. She only hoped Mr. Delacourte was a sound sleeper, and that the book lay on a table right next to the entrance.

When she reached his room, she checked the bottom of the door to see if any light seeped from the crack. All was darkness, so she tried the knob. She heard a tiny click and pushed. The door obliged by swinging open without a squeak. Holding her breath, she peeked inside.

Dade Delacourte lay on a king-size bed. A heavy masculine headboard constructed of oak, leather and hobnails climbed the rough-hewn wall above his head. The footboard was shorter, though just as substantial.

The massive bed was handsome and masculine, yet it paled in comparison to the man who lay there, a stirring vision in a silver pool of moonlight. He sprawled on his back, a forearm flung up, covering his eyes. His bear chest was all contoured muscle, his belly, washboard flat. Bathed in the pale beams of light, he appeared the image of a fallen Greek god.

A sheet was slung low across his hips, yet the moonlight disclosed one long leg stretched out, the other flung to the side, knee bent. There were other visible contours, thoroughly manly ones, that even in the cool of the night, made her cheeks burn. What did she think she was doing, ogling the man as he slept!

Tearing her gaze away, she scanned the room for

The Book. Nothing looked promising on the bedside table, just a watch and wallet. After a visual search, her glance was drawn back to him. This time she chanced to see an object near his hip, beneath a hand. The Book was open beneath his palm, as though he'd fallen asleep reading.

Why did his *hand* have to be on top of it? The Fates, it seemed, must have their fun. Perhaps this difficulty was their idea of payback for so easily allowing her access into Mr. Delacourte's life and home. The Fates were obviously telling Lauren she would not find the entire sojourn as simple as its beginning. As if today's diapering and feeding hardships weren't harassment enough!

This is no time to brood over your predicament, she told herself. *Get in there, swipe The Book and get out!*

Allowing herself no further wavering, Lauren slid inside and dropped to all fours. Her oversize T-shirt only went to her midthigh, so except for the occasional knee tramping on loose fabric, she scrambled to the bed with practically no sound. Her heartbeat roared in her ears, and it amazed her that the thundering didn't startle her boss awake. After a moment's uncertainty beside the bed, she peeked up to see if he'd moved.

No.

Good! She raised up higher, accidentally brushing the bedside table. The soft thud of something hitting the pine floor frightened her so badly she almost let out a shriek. Reflexively she ducked down, and spied what had dropped. Dade's wallet lay open on the floor. Her eyes had grown accustomed to the darkness, so even though the light was dim, she recognized a photograph, and picked up the wallet to get a closer look.

She could hardly believe her eyes. Mr. Delacourte carried a picture of himself in his wallet. She knew he was self-centered, but this was unbelievable. Highly annoyed, she flipped through the plastic card holders. *No other pictures.* Just laminated ID's that looked like membership cards to various professional organizations. She was surprised by some of them. Save The Whales and Save The Trees among other lofty ecological causes.

She closed the wallet, disconcerted with his hypocritical sense of value. He might care about the plight of whales and trees and the ozone, but he hadn't shown much consideration where Millie was concerned! Swallowing hard, she gingerly slid the billfold onto the bedside table. This was no time for anger; it was time for action.

Slowly she rose until she could see over the bed's surface, and The Book. It lay there, open, taunting her from beneath long fingers that appeared in the false light as though carved from marble. The bed was too big for her to snatch her objective from where she crouched. Did she dare put any weight on the mattress? How heavily did he sleep? What if he woke? What in the world would she say she was doing?

Never in a trillion years would he believe she was in there for any benign purpose—or that she'd walked in her sleep. He would assume she'd crawled into his bed for a quick little toss. He doubtless met women every day who were cool on the surface but hot-to-trot when the sun went down. He would never believe any nonsexual explanation. And she couldn't tell him the truth.

She sucked in a draught of courage, determining she had no choice but to try for it. She would get that book or die in the attempt!

Chewing her lower lip, she cautiously, breathlessly pressed on the bed with her elbows, making her way toward him. She advanced with the stealth of the hour hand on a clock, barely breathing, her movement scarcely detectable. She didn't dare go faster, for fear any jarring might wake him.

As her fingers grazed the precious book, he shifted. In the blink of an eye, Lauren found herself caught at the waist by the arm that had been covering his eyes. She instinctively opened her mouth, but managed not to scream, for the split second after he captured her, she sensed he was still asleep. She hadn't been discovered, after all—only trapped. Her relief was short-lived, as the reality of the situation made it to her brain.

Only trapped?

Only trapped!

Lauren lay there, petrified, her life flashing before her eyes. His lips hovered very close to her own. His eyelashes, long and thick, spread over high cheekbones. Even in these dire straits, Lauren found herself marveling at the moonlit beauty of the man-god, toppled from his pedestal in the Acropolis.

Lauren Smith! Her brain screamed. *Are you crazy? How can you even think of the man's face at a time like this! You're in bed with him, caught in his embrace. Get a grip! It can't get any worse than this!*

A heartbeat later, it did as he pulled her close. Her breasts were crushed against his chest. He was strong for a sleeping man. A small sound in his throat, a soft moan, had a strange, fluttery effect on her insides. His fingers spread across her lower back, and he rested his chin on the top of her head. She was so overwhelmed by her intimate imprisonment, her mind flew into the same state of chaos as her heart rate.

Warm, clean maleness radiated from him, which didn't ease her frenzied brain or pulse. Dade cuddled her like a lover! Only a thin sheet and her T-shirt separated them from—from flesh to flesh contact! Maybe Mr. Delacourte was accustomed to spending his nights entwined with his lover *du jour,* but Lauren wasn't!

She gulped and closed her eyes, throwing up a distraught prayer that she be delivered from this predicament. The Fates had to be laughing hysterically, now. Surely it was time to give her a break.

His big hand slipped lower to cup her hip, pulling her securely into him. Her heated reaction alarmed her, frightened her. He was so—so...

She squeezed her eyes tight, telling herself this was not happening. She was not here and she wasn't experiencing a wild, crazy desire for this inappropriate man. She had never met anyone she'd cared to have a serious relationship with, and this was no time to get hot and bothered. Of all the billions of men on earth, this was *not* the man for her!

He groaned softly, as though in awe. His lips brushed her hair in a kiss. Goodness! Was he dreaming about making love to someone? What if he woke up? What if he...

What would she...

Lauren stifled a whimper. If The Fates had any pity at all, they'd better give her that break—*now!*

CHAPTER FIVE

DADE woke with a start, and sat bolt upright. Frowning, he scanned his room as the fog of sleep lifted from his brain. What had made him wake up? The place was empty and utterly still, except for the distant whisper of the surf rushing to shore.

He detected an odd scent. Odd wasn't the right word. Unusual. Out of place. He sniffed the air. What was it? Honeysuckle? And oranges? What in the world would make him think he smelled honeysuckle and oranges in the dead of night? The scent seemed familiar, but he couldn't recall where he'd smelled it before. He yawned and ran a hand through his hair, strangely restless. Glancing out his patio doors, he noticed the sky to the east showed vague signs of dawn.

He leaned across his bed to read the luminous dial on his watch. Five minutes after five. He shook his head, experiencing a tug of wry humor. Since he was on vacation, he supposed he'd have to work at sleeping late. He wasn't accustomed to lounging around until five. Unfortunately today wouldn't be the day he learned about loafing. He felt edgy. He'd had an extraordinary dream—very real and very erotic.

He stared at his left hand. Why could he still feel the warmth and softness of a woman's ripe bottom in his palm? He never remembered dreams. And after he woke, their wispy remnants never perfumed the air or lingered on his skin.

With a testy growl, he rolled out of bed and tugged on a pair of jogging shorts. Maybe a run on the beach would ease his odd frustration. Clearly he'd been without female companionship too long. Perfecting and patenting his latest circuitry innovation had taken all his time and energy lately.

He needed to give his most recent lady-friend a call—assuming she was speaking to him. Eager for some distraction, he decided to invite a few friends out for an extended visit. His pledge to care for Joel's child didn't mean he had to turn himself into a monk.

Tina's whimpers woke Lauren at five-thirty. Staggering around like a zombie, she managed to change and dress the baby and get herself into the second of only three dresses she'd packed. She spent a good deal of her energy stifling yawns. What little sleep she might have had last night was spent in stark wakefulness, entwined in Dade Delacourte's arms.

His hands and body had been so intimately pressed against her that even now she hadn't recovered her normal pulse rate. She wondered how many zombies with racing hearts there were roaming the earth. She hoped very few, for the combination of being dead and goosey was not a happy one. Her eyes burned with the need to sleep, but her body prickled with a need for—for…

She tried not to allow herself to even *think* the word that described the need she felt, snuggled in Dade's arms. She didn't want to see Millie's side of her one-night stand with Dade. But Lauren had to admit, even if only to herself, the man was—well, to put it in Millie's lingo—*definitely do-able!*

Regretfully Lauren mused that if Dade held her in

his arms and was also *awake,* he would be hard to resist. The word "impossible" tried to intrude, but she forced back such racy lunacy. She was not here to *do* Dade Delacourte. She was here to find legally arguable evidence that would allow her to win custody of Tina away from her sexy, er, lecherous father!

At six-thirty the sun was crawling up, up into the morning sky, dazzling the sea and spreading welcome heat. Out on the sunny deck, Lauren rocked Tina in her arms, and inhaled the freshness of a day that held all the earmarks of perfection.

If only she and Tina were in Oklahoma, sitting on the small balcony of her apartment. The view of the complex parking lot would be less spectacular, but even so, it would be perfect. There was only one stumbling block to this flawless vision, and that was Dade Delacourte. Lauren gazed at her precious niece, drowsing in her arms. Tiny lips pursed as if taking her bottle, though it was set empty on a nearby, glass-topped table.

Careful not to disturb the child, Lauren unearthed The Book from its hiding place at the edge of her seat cushion, and began to read. Her chances to grab precious minutes to absorb baby-care knowledge had been so sporadic, she hadn't made it through Chapter One. Speed-scanning the pages as she was, she had strong doubts she would catch all the important details.

Dade would miss The Book sooner or later, so she'd have to put it back. Not in his room, however. Lauren decided she'd drop it somewhere in the living room or kitchen. He could just torment himself about his patchy memory, for all she cared. She was *not* sneaking back into his bedroom in the middle of the night. She didn't even plan to venture onto the second floor, again!

"Hi there!"

Lauren jumped at the sound of Dade's voice, and quickly slipped the book into its hiding place. She shifted toward the beach as he ran up to the house amid dunes and sea grass. He waved and grinned. Reflexively she lifted an arm, but her attention was drawn to something behind him. She squinted. It looked like a dog or a very big cat.

Dade took the steps two at a time. Lauren was disconcerted to notice that he wore nothing but a pair of black shorts. Or were they swim trunks? Whichever, his scant attire was recklessly inconsiderate. How dare he advance on her with such potent, tomcat grace and bronze, shiny muscles. How did he expect her pulse to get back to its usual, sane tempo, if he strutted around practically naked! She wondered if "practically naked" was grounds for...

She heaved a disgruntled sigh. Probably not. Too many perfectly good daddies wore shorts and swim trunks for it to be actionable.

He hit the deck and slowed to a walk. Much to Lauren's chagrin, he headed straight for her. "How's it going?" he asked quietly.

"Fine." She caught sight of his shaggy shadow as it clambered onto the deck behind him. "What's that?"

Dade placed his hands on trim hips and shifted to look back. He took in a gulp of air and his chest expanded engagingly. Lauren chastised herself for staring, and forced her attention to the dog. "He followed me home." The mutt trotted up to Dade, its tail wagging up a storm, its tongue lolling. For a shaggy, sandy creature, it was cute, all beige, one dark eye hidden by fur. Dade knelt and stroked the dog's back. "No collar. He feels a little thin. I'll put an ad in the local paper, just in case he's lost and not dumped." He glanced at Lauren. "Meanwhile, what do you think we should call him?"

She was taken aback by the question. She hadn't expected Dade Delacourte to give a fig about stray animals. "Call him?"

He gave the dog a quick once-over. "What do you think about Spike?"

"Spike?" Still confused, she frowned. "Well—first of all it looks more like a Fluffy than a Spike, and second, why would you call him anything?"

Dade glanced at her, a brow lifting. "If nobody claims him, I'll keep him."

Lauren was stunned. "Why?"

His lips curled in a crooked grin. "What a question. What would you have me do. Run him off?"

She stared. This was an ironic idiosyncrasy in his character. He took in stray dogs, but abandoned his own offspring, unless forced to deal with them! "Yes," she said seriously. "I suppose that is what I expected you to do."

His brow furrowed, but his grin didn't disappear. He looked at her as though trying to decipher what made her such a cold, uncaring being. "Not an animal lover, huh?"

She removed her gaze to the baby, censure clamoring at her lips. How dare *he*—of all the hypocritical jerks on earth—look at her with a jaundiced eye! "I'm very fond of animals," she muttered. "However, it pains me to meet someone who cares more for a stray dog than his own child."

When he didn't respond, she peered his way. Powerful arm and shoulder muscles coiled and stretched as he stroked the dog. "Have you met many like that in your work, Quinn?" The quiet remark pulled her gaze to his face. He glanced her way, his expression closed, unreadable.

"Not many," she said, unsmiling. Her eyes remained locked with his, her silence eloquently telling.

His lashes dropped to half-mast, as though he was striving to see into her brain. After a minute, his lips twitched. "Fluffy, you think?" His abrupt change of subject took her off guard. "That's a cruel name for a macho boy dog, Miss Quinn." He grinned his dimpled grin. *Talk about cruel!* "What do you say we compromise and call him Spikey?"

She blinked, irritated by his offhandedness. Surely he'd received her unspoken condemnation! Was he so unfeeling he could slough it off without a twinge of guilt, or was he merely thickheaded? No, he wasn't stupid. She'd read about him—Dade Delacourte, the electronic genius with a dozen patents, drawing in a king's ransom every year. She shrugged, disconcerted and depressed. Why did she have to find such a despicable bum even vaguely attractive? "Spikey's fine, sir," she mumbled.

"Dade." He stood. "I'll call the newspaper office, then I'll give ol' Spikey a bath. Afterward, we can talk."

She shot him a panicked glance. "Talk?" The word came out in a squeak, and she cleared the dismay from her throat. *"You—and me?"*

He indicated Tina. "Remember? Questions? Hands-on?"

She remembered all too well—*his hands on her.*

Her cheeks sizzled with mortification. That's *not* what he meant. He didn't even know his hands had been on her. "Oh, right..." She ducked her head, pretending to check Tina's diaper. "Whenever you sex, sir."

"What?"

She cringed. Did she say that out loud! "Whenever you *Dade*—sir. I mean, whenever you say, Dade."

Heavenly days, man, put on some clothes!

Dade headed downstairs with a freshly bathed and dried Spikey at his heels. The dog wasn't the only clean male on the stairs, since Dade had showered and donned shorts and a knit shirt. "Now, boy, how about some food?" He grinned at the dog, its bushy tail fanning the air like a windshield wiper set on Frantic. Halfway down the steps he heard music and stopped. Spikey ran down a couple more steps before he realized his beloved savior had stilled. He looked back at Dade, then moved up the steps to sit beside him.

Dade noticed the mutt's movement, but on a peripheral level. His major attention was on the woman at the far end of the Great Room. She sat before his grand piano, playing a lilting Cole Porter standard. Tina lay on her back on a baby quilt that had been spread over an oriental rug. She played with her feet, nearly succeeding at getting one complete set of toes into her mouth.

Dade watched the baby for another moment, his brows dipping at the reminder of how his life had been altered by Joel's reckless lifestyle. He inhaled, reminding himself that it was much too late for regrets.

His gaze lifted to Quinn as she played. In her

hands, the music drifted across the air as he was sure Cole Porter had meant it to. "Very pretty," he called, making his way down the rest of the steps.

She froze and the music abruptly halted. He shook his head. "Don't stop on my account. I'm gratified to have such a multifaceted nanny."

Her cheeks colored, but her face took on that stony expression he couldn't quite fathom. Why did she turn into granite every time he walked in the room? What had he done that was so contemptible to make her hide her softer side from him?

"I—I found some sheet music in the bench," she said.

He walked over and lounged against the piano. "It was my father's. He left it to me."

"Oh? Do you play?"

He shook his head. "I was more into math than music."

"But your father played?" She shifted to glance at the page before her. Though she didn't give any outward signs, Dade sensed she was nervous.

"Just for fun."

She didn't meet his eyes. "And your mother?"

"I have no idea." He didn't mean for his reply to come out so grim. He was surprised that even after all these years he could still feel so strongly about the subject of his mother. On the positive side, his tone had the effect of drawing Quinn's gaze.

"I don't understand," she said.

"My mother wasn't much into—responsibility. She left us before I got to know her."

The nanny's brows knit for an instant, then her dour mask shifted into place. She didn't respond, merely stared at the sheet music.

"Go ahead and play."

She cast him an uncertain glance. "I—I *do* think music is good for the baby."

He smiled, not quite sure why. "Dr. Wickerbasket's theories, again?"

For a second, she seemed on the verge of smiling, and Dade found himself holding his breath. "Actually it's—" She cut herself off and glanced sharply in the direction of the baby. Her moss-green eyes flashed with alarm.

Dade spun in time to see Spikey sniff Tina's uplifted foot. The baby cackled, and stretched out both feet in an effort to make contact with the dog. Spikey sprang back, plainly opting to give the noisy creature a wide berth. He beat a path to Dade and plopped down at his feet.

"Maybe I should hold the dog?" he asked, facing Quinn.

"Maybe you should hold the baby." Her expression was stiff, the lurking smile gone.

Experiencing a surge of misgiving, he nodded. "Right." He bent and lifted Tina into his arms. It always surprised him how little she weighed, how tiny she was. Carefully he held her against his chest. Patting her back, he turned to Quinn. "Please, play."

She looked stiffer than she had a minute before, and Dade expected her to decline. When she began to thumb through some of the sheet music on the bench beside her, the strangest sense of gratification rushed through him.

"I always enjoy Liszt's 'Consolation No. 3 in D-flat Major,'" she said. "Would you like to hear that?"

He laughed softly. She might as well have been

speaking in ancient Greek for all he knew about the selection. Before he could voice his thought, he was startled to hear Tina's cackle. She swatted his chin and babbled gaily. He grinned at Quinn. "I believe that was a yes."

The nanny nodded, scanned the music, then looked back at him. "Why don't you sit down?"

He'd never actually sat and held his niece before, so the suggestion caught him by surprise. He wasn't comfortable with the idea, but *blast it,* what was this month for? He needed to learn how to care for the child, and that included knowing how to hold her and comfort her with actual physical contact. He set his jaw with determination. "Sure. Why not?"

He took a seat in a nearby easy chair. Spikey sprang to his feet and followed to curl up beside his outstretched legs. Quinn began to play softly, her fingers drifting over the keys. Dade judiciously adjusted the baby in his arms as Quinn produced from a bunch of black lines and squiggles on a page, a lovely, almost unearthly melody.

After a few minutes, Dade noticed Tina had stilled and was watching his face. He tucked in his chin so he could get a better look at her expression. When he did, she grinned and patted his cheek.

He felt a curious tug in his gut and looked away. His gaze fell on Quinn's profile. Her back wasn't as stiff as before. Her hands, slender, graceful, glided along, fingers dancing on the keys. The soft, lush composition filled the ear and the air with such soothing strains, Dade found himself relaxing.

His attention lifted from her hands to her face, and he was stunned by what he saw. Transformed by the music, Quinn was, quite simply, a beautiful woman.

He stared, as she coaxed the sensual strains from the instrument, amazed by how the morning sunlight struck her hair, illuminating it with unrestrained drama. Suddenly the chestnut-brown was ablaze with auburn highlights. He'd never particularly noticed her hair, but now hc realized it was dazzling, thick and shiny. And tempting.

He felt a lurch in his gut. Tempting? He swallowed and winced. *Not a chance, Delacourte. She's an employee. There are rules about these things.*

He made himself look away, scanned the scene, making every effort to do so with his usual detachment. Unfortunately his gaze was drawn back to Quinn. That damnable golden sunshine haloed her as she performed, her body swaying to the music. Her features were tender, her cheeks a radiant pink. A sweet smile graced her lips. *Good Lord.* He wished he had never seen her responsive side. The old saying, "Be careful what you wish for...." came to him, and he frowned at its insidious accuracy.

Tina stroked his chin and cooed, as though attempting to sing along. The sweet nonsense lent a quaint charm to the classical composition. Dade stared down at the child as she jabbered and gurgled. His infant niece had no idea the world could be anything other than music and kindness. How innocent she was. He prayed she would never know the death of Joel, her father, and her unexpected appearance in Dade's life, caused pain and guilt that stalked him relentlessly. If he could keep that from her, perhaps one day he could begin to forgive himself for all the things he *hadn't* done.

His gaze trailed from Quinn to Tina to the scruffy mongrel at his feet. It was almost as though Dade

Delacourte had been dropped by aliens into this idyllic likeness of a Norman Rockwell painting, entitled *The Loving Family Unit.*

Blast! Of all the bizarre parodies in the world, there could be none more freakish than this. His lips twisted ruefully. A discarded mutt, a nanny who disliked him and a baby, shoved into his hesitant care, were a far cry from anyone's definition of a loving family!

Dade wondered if Norman Rockwell would find the irony amusing.

''Bathing the Baby'' was in Chapter Three of The Book. Lauren hadn't had a chance to read it, yet. She wanted desperately to grab some time to herself to go over that section, before she would have to bathe the baby in front of Dade. Her first attempt at bathing Tina had been in private, but with very unsatisfactory results. Her niece had splashed and kicked so much Lauren was soaked to the skin.

At least, she'd learned not to support Tina's head in the crook of her elbow. That got Lauren too close to the water. She decided she'd try supporting Tina's head with one hand, placing her farther away. Harder to splash.

That had been a lovely daydream. Her newest inspiration was going no better. Water flew everywhere as Tina kicked and cackled and splashed in the pink oval tub that sat beside the sink on the bathroom counter.

''She's having a good time.'' Dade's voice was ripe with laughter. ''The question is, are you?''

Lauren cleared soap from her eyes with the back of her wrist, grateful baby shampoo didn't sting. She licked her lips, and was immediately sorry. Baby shampoo may not cause tears, but it tasted horrible. "Uh, a child, of this age..." she began, trying to sound knowledgeable in the face of a chubby-laughing-little-human-outboard-motor, "is exploring the tacti—*petooie*..." She spat out a dollop of soap that had been hurled onto her tongue.

"I get it, Quinn," Dade said, laughing outright. "Maybe it would be best if you kept your mouth closed."

She peered at him. He was by no means Mr. Totally-Dry, himself. His knit shirt hadn't been spared either soap splatters or the occasional deluge by tiny flailing feet. "The main thing," she went on, trying not to grimace at the soapy taste in her mouth, "is that you don't allow her head to go under, or she'll get water up her nose."

"But it's okay if she kicks water up mine?"

"Absolutely!" She bit her lip, deciding she shouldn't have sounded so enthusiastic. "I mean—you're a big boy." *Yes, he certainly is!* the unruly imp in her brain teased. "You can handle it," she finished, trying to sound businesslike. "A child Tina's age might choke."

She carefully ran the washcloth over Tina's forehead, squeezing out water so it would rinse soap from the fine, blond hair, but not run down her face. She bent lower, concentrating on rinsing the hair clean, as Tina grabbed the front of her dress. Sadly it was a button-front style, and the baby's tug was all that was necessary for the small round buttons to slip from the holes. In one brief instant Lauren's dress suddenly gaped open to the waist.

Her turquoise bra hadn't been meant for outerwear, and when it became exposed Lauren froze. Tina was so delighted with her triumph, she went into a kicking frenzy. Splashes of pure hilarity soaked Lauren's bra to near invisibility. Her initial reaction was to drop the baby and run, but her natural maternal instincts took over.

She held the baby's head and neck with one hand while trying to work the top button back into its hole with the other. After two failed attempts, she couldn't stifle a frustrated moan. She'd never realized that one-handed buttoning was so difficult—especially when fingers were slippery with soap-bubbles.

"Would you like some help with those?" It was clear Dade had attempted to wipe the humor from his tone, but he hadn't been totally successful.

Mortified beyond words, she ground out, "For your sake, *those* had better be a reference to the *buttons!*" Her breasts, only slightly hazy behind thin, soaked blue nylon, were exposed to the man's view! She shot him a lethal glare. "As for helping me, you could *leave!*"

He cleared his throat, his lips quirking. "Why don't I take the baby?" As he spoke he stepped close and lay his hand under hers, behind Tina's head. "You can..." He halted, then seemed to sniff her hair. "Honeysuckle—and oranges?" he murmured. "Is that you?"

At a time like this, why was the man babbling about her herbal shampoo? She ducked back to better see his face. *"Excuse me?"* A split second after she spoke, she realized her dress gaped right under his nose, now. *Stupid, stupid woman!* She hunched forward. "Just—just take her, *please!*"

"I've got her," he said quietly. "You can let go."

Lauren's jaws were clamped so tightly she was

afraid her teeth would crumble. She released her niece, allowing Dade to take her. When she was sure the baby's face wasn't going to sink below the surface, she whirled away. Hands trembling, she began to refasten her dress. Her idiotic trembly fingers fumbled so badly the job seemed to take forever.

She heard splashing and gurgling.

"Whoa, young lady," Dade said. "Soapy washcloths do not go in the mouth."

After she finally got the buttons to obey, she remained facing away for a long moment while she breathed deeply to gather her poise. How was she going to face the man? Why did she have to wear that skimpy bra today? Why didn't she have on her industrial-strength bra? Why did the dratted baby food have to soak through her dress last night, and force her to throw the big, white cotton bra in with her other laundry? Why were the Fates bent on making her pay dearly for her deception?

She closed her eyes and sucked in one more deep breath. *Be calm, Lauren,* she told herself. *The man has seen plenty of women's underwear. And plenty of female breasts—no doubt heaving and quivering in eager anticipation.*

Her face burned, and she tried to rein in her depraved thoughts. This kind of thinking was totally unlike her!

"How are you coming, Quinn?"

His question startled her so badly, she threw her hand to her heart. It took her several swallows to gain control of her voice. "I'm fine," she said, thinly.

"I think she's clean." His deep laugher filled the small room and echoed around them. "I know I am."

Keeping her gaze averted, Lauren busied herself

laying out an infant towel. "Lift her gently out of the tub, and I'll take over." As Lauren smoothed out the fluffy hooded terrycloth, she was chagrined to see her hands shake.

Dade lifted Tina out and lay her on the towel. Lauren noticed he peered at her hands for a moment. It was only then that she realized she gripped the edge of the tile counter as if it were her last handhold to prevent a plunge into a pit of cranky rattlesnakes. He made no comment, and went about folding the towel around the baby. "Why don't I dry her, Quinn?" he asked. "I have a pretty good grasp of what towels do."

She sensed he'd detected her agitation over the soaked bra incident, and was giving her an out—a little space to get over it. Amazingly sensitive of him, considering the heartless scoundrel he was. "Very well," she said crisply. "When you're through drying her, wrap her in the towel and take her out to the changing table. I'll get her night things ready."

"Check."

At the bathroom door, Lauren paused and looked back to make sure he wasn't doing anything stupid, like using the towel as though he was buffing a shoe. He gingerly patted the infant with it as she giggled and gurgled at him.

His expression had gone serious, almost haunted. His jaw muscles bunched. She frowned at the sight. Haunted? A quick, harsh thought stiffened her spine against any softening for the man. From the troubled look on his face, these fledgling attempts to learn to care for Tina wouldn't last long. Probably not even to the end of the week. She'd overheard him tell

Goodberry of plans to invite friends up for an extended visit.

Lauren experienced a surge of grim satisfaction.

Let the debauchery begin!

CHAPTER SIX

TOMORROW was Friday and Dade's guests would be arriving. Lauren didn't know what kind of debauchery the master of the house usually indulged in, but Goodberry and Braga had been behaving very strangely all afternoon. Dade had gone into the small, nearby town with Spikey to buy the dog a collar and run a few other personal errands. She presumed he was stocking up on whips and chains and sex oils, or whipping cream, or whatever perverse sexual aids he might need for his wild beach orgies.

Not long after he left, Goodberry and Braga carried his king-size mattress and box springs down to the beach. Now, much to Lauren's astonishment, they doused them with gasoline and set them on fire. She observed the bizarre scene from the deck, with one ear open for cries from Tina. The infant was taking her afternoon nap. She usually slept for a solid hour, but considering Lauren's limited experience as her so-called nanny, she was insecure and constantly on edge.

Not only that, Dade had found The Book and had returned it to his room. Lauren had half a notion to dash up there while he was gone and grab it, but she couldn't quite bring herself to. Dade couldn't help being suspicious by now, finding the thing in all manner of odd places where he *knew* he hadn't left it. She didn't dare chance it again.

Besides, she'd already been forced to make up

most of her child-care rules—giving the fictional Dr. Wickle Wickerburger credit. She hoped Dade didn't try to find Dr. Wickerburger's reference work in the local bookstore, or she would be unmasked as a fraud. She stared at Braga and Goodberry as flames and black smoke billowed out of the bedding. What kind of kinky craziness was this?

A whimper coming from the remote device on her belt made her spring away from the rail. Tina was awake and hungry for her afternoon bottle. After almost a week, Lauren was becoming accustomed to her niece's schedule, and had the formula warming. After gathering up the fussy baby and changing her, she took the bottle and baby onto the deck to sit in the shade and watch the weird mattress burning ritual.

Tina was half finished with her formula when the door to the Great Room opened. Without looking Lauren knew Dade was back. She heard the creak of redwood as he approached. The tap-tap-tap of Spikey's paws pitter-patted closer and closer too.

"What in *hell* is going on?"

She looked at him. His attention was focused on the bed bonfire.

"They're burning your mattress," Lauren said, wondering at his apparent surprise. "Didn't you tell them to?"

He flicked a narrowed glance her way. "Why in blazes would I tell them to burn my mattress?"

She was as blank as he appeared to be. "I don't know. I figured it was some kind of—party thing."

His frown deepened as he glared at her. "Party thing?"

"Well—your guests are arriving tomorrow, aren't they?"

He nodded, his jaws bunching. "Yes. And you think burning my mattress is part of preparing for guests?"

She was confused. "Isn't it?"

He dragged a hand through his hair. "Is it the way *you* prepare for guests where you come from?"

She felt a little stupid. He seemed truly incredulous. "Uh—no."

He lifted his chin in a half nod. "Really? Well, strange as it may seem, Miss Quinn, neither do I." He flicked his gaze to the beach and stalked to the rail. "*Goodberry!* What are you doing?"

Both figures on the beach spun to face him. "I can explain, sir!" came Goodberry's shout.

"I damn well hope so!"

The portly man had rolled up his pant legs and taken off his shoes and socks. Grabbing them, he shambled toward the house. Braga didn't move. It surprised Lauren to realize that the cook, for all her intimidating severity, seemed more fainthearted about facing her boss than Goodberry did. Lauren had seen the woman chasing the manservant around with a spatula, shouting in her native Portuguese. Dade had laughingly called it "foreplay." The two seemed an unlikely pair, but love or lust or whatever the relationship might be, could rarely be explained with logic.

Clearly Goodberry had more intestinal fortitude and pluck than Lauren gave him credit for, considering the jovial smile that rode his lips as he approached his fuming employer. Maybe Goodberry had something on Dade, and had him under his blackmailer's thumb. This seemed likely, considering the rogue Dade was.

Goodberry huffed and puffed up the stairs; a smile continued to ride his lips. "Good afternoon, sir," he said. "I trust your trip into town was successful."

"The trip was fine, Goodberry. Now tell me—*why* in Hades are you burning my mattress?"

The servant's expression altered to a fascinating combination of pity and deference. "It's not what it looks like, sir."

"Thank goodness, since it looks like you're burning my mattress." Lauren watched Dade's grim profile as he folded his arms before him. "Since it's not what it looks like, what *exactly* is it?"

"I am burning your mattress and box springs, sir, but entirely out of necessity."

Dade's jaw muscles knotted. "I have five guests coming tomorrow, and you found it necessary to burn *my* mattress today?"

"Yes, sir." Goodberry's brows wrinkled with what looked like sympathy. "You see, it was contaminated."

Lauren was startled by the word. "Contaminated?" She didn't realize she'd spoken aloud until both men turned to look at her.

After a second, Dade jerked back to stare at Goodberry. "What do you mean, contaminated?"

"Your bed was stricken with an infestation of fiber-eating mites, sir. It had to be destroyed."

"My..." Dade's face went hard. "Are you nuts, man?"

"Simply doing my job, sir." Goodberry smiled politely. "I've ordered another bed."

Dade's expression eased. "Good. When will it arrive?"

"Two weeks—possibly three."

A flush of color rose under Dade's skin. *"Two weeks?"*

"Possibly three." Goodberry remained as composed as if he were telling his boss the weather was pleasant.

"*Dammit,* man! Where do you propose Allegra and I—" He broke off the question and inhaled through flaring nostrils. After a second he seemed to get hold of himself. "Where do you propose I sleep?"

Goodberry remained poised and unruffled beneath his boss's harsh glare. "I'll put on my thinking cap, sir."

"Do that!"

"Right away, sir." Goodberry indicated his shoes. "I believe I should get to the laundry now, if you'll excuse me?"

Dade jerked his head toward the house. "Go." As he watched his servant shuffle off, he pushed both hands through his hair, visibly furious.

Lauren observed his face, struck that even closed in an ominous expression, his dark eyes and firm mouth held an eerily sensuous appeal. "I knew he disliked Allegra, but..." His gaze darted to her, as though he just remembered he wasn't alone. With a slight sideways motion of his jaw and a blink, she could tell he worked to get his anger under control. Those great lips quirked in his effort to conceal his anger. "How's Tina, Quinn?"

Lauren was startled by his quick transformation and nodded. "She's fine, sir."

"Dade." He managed a full-fledged grin, and it affected her badly. With one last glance at his burning bed, he bent to pet Spikey. The mutt sported his brand-new collar and tags. "Remind me not to go into town, boy.'' He glanced at Lauren in time to see her grin. ''So you think my burning bed is funny?'' A brow rose and his grin grew wry, yet it was hard to squelch her smile in the face of it—wry or otherwise. His smiles were treacherously catching.

She shook her head and adjusted her face. ''No, sir—Dade. It's certainly not funny.''

''Liar.'' He snorted and shook his head. ''If Goodberry hadn't been with the family for thirty years...'' He glanced away. ''Hell!''

Lauren watched him as he turned to the dog and stroked its fur. She sensed he didn't believe fiber-eating mites had contaminated his mattress. And Lauren had to admit, she'd never heard of such an animal. It seemed rather obvious that Goodberry didn't like Dade's current girlfriend, and he'd taken it upon himself in a not-very-subtle effort to keep him from sleeping with her. This was a strange twist to the ''Dade Delacourte Debauchery Story.'' She wondered where he and his current ladylove would sleep, now, and she used the word *sleep* loosely.

She felt a shiver run up her spine and wondered at the reason. Surely the fact that Mr. Delacourte would be having wild sex with one or more women over the weekend didn't upset her! Surely she wasn't feeling a twinge of jealous...*Lauren Smith,* she screamed inwardly, *he is not a nice man. He might take in stray mutts and care about the environment, but that doesn't make him nice! At least not where women are concerned, and the last time you looked, you were one!*

Tina finished her formula, so Lauren lifted her to her shoulder to burp her. Without the slightest desire to, she continued to watch Dade stroke Spikey's back.

She noticed his hand, his long fingers, and had the arrant longing to know their gentle warmth again, of being pressed close to him—

No! she warned herself. *Remember why you're here! You're trying to catch him in his debauchery, not join him!*

There was something very different about Dade's evenings lately. Before dinner, it had become his habit to retire to the Great Room where Quinn played the piano. Spikey curled beside his easy chair as he supported Tina against his chest. Tonight, as Dade lounged there with Tina tugging at his lower lip, he marveled at how ridiculously cozy the room seemed.

Quinn had taken it upon herself to strap the baby to her back and take afternoon walks along the dunes, picking wildflowers and interesting grasses. Due to her efforts, quaint bouquets splashed homey color all over the place. It reminded him of his grandparents' home and the summers he and Joel spent there. It was odd how a little music and a smattering of wildflowers could change the complexion of a place. Not since he'd painstakingly had his grandparents' barn moved piece by piece to his seaside property had it felt like a refuge from the corporate jungle. Not until now.

He glanced at Quinn as she played "Buttons and Bows," a humorous show tune. She sang along to her own accompaniment. Though she didn't have an operatic voice, she had a very pleasant one.

"You're very good," he said. "Is your family musical?"

"Not really." She didn't turn his way and continued to play. "I took up the piano because my sister needed accompaniment. She has a wonderful voice and loved to entertain as a child."

"Where is your sister, now?"

Quinn fumbled, causing a sour note, but she rapidly recovered. "We're not close. I—I'm not really sure where she is." She stumbled over another chord, bit her lip, then got herself back to speed. He watched her solemnly for a moment. The subject of Quinn's sister plainly upset her. Thoughts of Joel shot through Dade's consciousness and he winced. He wasn't the only person in the world with sibling troubles and regrets. "She must have an exceptional singing voice, because yours is very nice," he said, trying to keep the mood light.

She inhaled deeply. *Damn.* He'd made her self-conscious, touched on a hot-button. Her sister. Interesting that his little nanny and he had a common sorrow. He would remember not to mention her singing, or her sister. He preferred it when Quinn allowed herself to be soft and real. The only time he saw that part of her was when she let herself open up with the music.

Tina babbled in a singsong way, seeming to want to take up where Quinn left off. As she gabbled, she seized his nose.

"Hey! It's 'Buttons and Bows,' not 'Buttons and *Nose,*' young lady." He grinned at her. "Lay off the beak."

She gurgled and smiled.

He looked down at her as she patted his jaw. As she'd shown on other occasions she seemed intrigued by the slight roughness of his five-o'clock shadow, and leaned her face into his jaw. She nuzzled his chin with her nose; her forehead brushed his mouth. She smelled nice—lightly sweet, like talcum powder. With a cackle, she lurched back and presented him with a wide, toothless grin. Then both little hands came up and patted him on either side of his jaw.

His lips twitched, then he chuckled. There was a quality about his niece unlike anything he'd experienced. Though he tried, he couldn't remain resistant to it. He was unable to put a name to what it was, but in the presence of this innocent being, he felt strangely at peace. Maybe it was the renewal of life a baby represented, of the potential, he was drawn to. The chance to begin again, to make things right. Pay a debt.

He gently nipped at Tina's fingers with his teeth, eliciting from her a riot of giggles as she yanked her hand away. Almost instantly, she stuck her fingers back into his mouth for another chance to get his teeth to play with her. When he nipped, she burst out in unrestrained baby laughter that was so infectious he chuckled.

"What's going on?"

Quinn's question caused Dade to glance toward the piano. She stopped playing and turned toward them, looking puzzled. He pulled his head back to free his mouth from questing fingers. "I'm not sure. I think we're playing something called 'Bite My Digits.'"

"Oh, really?" She folded her hands in her lap and stared, her expression serious. "I'm not sure Dr. Wickerbasket would approve."

He flicked a glance her way. "Dr. Wicker*basket?*"

Her cheeks took on a pleasant flush. "*Burger.* I believe I said Wickerburger. The mouth is a breeding ground for germs."

"I believe you said—" His comment was cut off

when Tina thrust her hand into his mouth. He nipped her fingers and she pulled her hand away, squealing with delight. "Wicker*basket,* Quinn." He grinned, not sure where the urge came from. "And for your information, my oral hygiene has never been questioned."

"As the baby's nanny it's my duty to express my concerns."

"About my mouth?"

"I have a duty—to see that my, uh, charge remains healthy."

He noticed how thoroughly she avoided eye contact, and was both amused and annoyed by her prim reserve. She gave no hint of it, but Dade sensed fire raging beneath that austere facade. Suddenly, irrationally, he wanted a glimpse. "I assure you, Miss Quinn, no one who has ever come into contact with my mouth has become ill because of it. If you care to make a test, I'm at your service." He made a bet with himself that he would soon see how pink her cheeks could get. With the wry lift of a brow and a teasing grin, he added, "To glean the most credible results, I suggest we include tongues."

Her lips formed a horrified "oh" and she swallowed several times. She was clearly so overwhelmed she could neither move nor speak. Her cheeks actually glowed—a charming display of bright pink. He cleared his throat. He was a little sorry he'd kidded her, though he'd certainly gotten the reaction he wanted. "It was a joke, Quinn."

She blinked, seeming to come out of her daze. "What?"

"A joke." He felt like a jerk. He hadn't meant to make her so uncomfortable. *Sure, you did, jackass!*

Now apologize! "It wasn't a great joke," he said. "I'm sorry."

"I—I only meant..."

"I know what you meant, Quinn." He pushed up from the chair. "Let's forget it. Now if you'll take Tina, I'm going to wash up for dinner."

She accepted the baby without comment, averting her gaze. "By the way, the flowers are nice," he said in another attempt to make amends, however lame. "Thanks for brightening up this old barn."

She flitted a glance his way and he grinned, striving to hold her gaze.

She nodded, but promptly severed eye contact. Moving her attention to Tina, she cuddled the baby to her breast. "Tina needs changing," she mumbled. "Excuse me." She scooted out the far side of the bench, an obvious effort to keep from skimming too near him. Dade watched as she scurried across the room, then disappeared down the hall.

Annoyed at himself, he mouthed a curse. What was his problem, taunting Quinn with the suggestion that they kiss? And *tongues,* yet! Was he nuts? She was the nanny, for heaven's sake! It was a good thing Allegra was coming tomorrow. She would ease his physical frustrations.

A thought struck and he frowned. "Except, I have no damn bed!"

Lauren dashed into her room and came to a stumbling halt at what she saw. Goodberry stood beside her bed, holding her open purse. When he heard her, he turned, his expression dour.

"What—what are you doing?" she choked out, panic shoving her heart in her throat.

He closed her purse and placed it on the bed, his expression showed no remorse at having been caught rifling through her belongings. He faced her. "Forgive me, miss," he said quietly. "I have a duty to Master Dade."

She frowned. "To *snoop?*"

His smile seemed uncommonly benevolent, considering the circumstances. She'd been caught as the fake and liar she was. "I—I can explain!" she said, then blanched. *She could?*

"Please do." He inclined his head as though prepared to listen.

She swallowed. What did she think she was going to say? In her leisure hours she worked as a government spy—that the ID she carried was fake? *Lauren Smith, this isn't a movie thriller. It's your life, and it's falling to ruins! Think!*

Her drawn-out silence was equivalent to a confession. She was good and caught! Nothing she could say now would change that.

"To be frank, miss," he said, at last, "I admit, I overheard you talking to the baby earlier today. You called yourself 'Aunt Lauren.'" His expression took on an air of genuine sympathy. "Knowing the child's middle name is Lauren, I put two and two together, and decided to investigate further." He indicated her purse. "According to the driver's license with your picture, a teacher's ID and a library card, it seems your name is Lauren Smith and you teach music in a school in Oklahoma. In the presence of these facts, I have come to the unhappy conclusion you are *not* Madeline Quinn, the nanny Mr. Delacourte hired."

The evidence was certainly incriminating! Lauren spiraled into a chasm of loss, only able to hold back a wail of grief with Herculean effort. She loved Tina. She'd loved her from the first glimpse she'd had of the baby. Suddenly all her plans had been slammed into a brick wall—the end of her relationship with Tina—a relationship that in only days had become so vital a separation would ravage her heart. Tina was a part of her, now. Her family. She flailed around in her mind for anything—any truth or excuse...even a lie—that would keep Goodberry's silence! "Please—"

"Naturally it's my obligation to report what I've found to Mr. Delacourte," the servant interjected.

"Oh—but..." Bile rose in her throat and she tasted bitter defeat, ruthlessly torn from Tina's life, now that the damning evidence against Mr. Delacourte was only *hours* away! What could she do? What possible appeal might still his tongue? *Money?* She didn't have any money! Besides, would a bribe even work? If he had been with the family for thirty years—even to assume he could be bought was ludicrous.

She tried to maintain her fragile control, but felt quivery and feeble. For the baby's sake she stumbled to the changing table and lay Tina down, afraid if she didn't she might drop her.

As she moved, her thoughts scrambled for solid purchase. If not bribery, then what? *Threats?* No, she had nothing to threaten the man with. *Think, Lauren! Think!*

She turned to face him, surprised at the compassion in his eyes. Compassion? Yes, he was a man of great compassion. She'd sensed that from their first meeting. Although he revered his master, perhaps she could use his compassionate nature to her advantage. She chose her words carefully. "Goodberry," she whispered, "you've found me out. It's true. I am Tina's aunt. I searched for my sister for months, worrying myself sick about the baby."

She didn't try to hide the tears that filled her eyes at the recollection. "My sister ran off when she was nine months pregnant. She didn't want the baby. I didn't know it then, but I understand now Millie wanted to get revenge, then to get back to Hollywood to chase her dreams of fame. I only found out Mr. Delacourte had custody of Tina the day before I came to New York. When I tried to see him at his office, they said he was leaving on a month-long vacation."

A tear fell. An honest tear. It was a shame she was about to pollute the purity of her emotions with a lie. "I—I wanted to see my niece, to make sure she was all right. I'd heard of Mr. Delacourte. I knew Tina could have everything, growing up in such a man's home. But I had to see for myself that she was being cared for."

Lauren halted, mixed feelings surging through her—love for Tina, fear of losing her, and shame at the need to lie. Clasping her hands in a pleading gesture, she whispered urgently, "I—when I arrived, everyone mistook me for the nanny. Suddenly I was whisked off to spend a month with Tina. I—I couldn't believe my luck. All I wanted was to know she was all right, and all at once I was holding her. I was given the unbelievable gift of being with her! I—I couldn't—I'd been looking for her, agonizing for so long—I couldn't bring myself to tell Mr. Delacourte he'd made a mistake!"

Her emotions warring, she stared at him. Another tear slid down her cheek. "I wasn't planning to steal her away in the middle of the night." That was true.

Lauren had always planned to get Tina legally, through the courts. "Besides, now that you know who I am and where I live, I couldn't possibly get away with such a plan."

She blinked, releasing more tears. Goodberry remained quiet, looking worried. His own eyes glittered with moisture.

"I just want to spend this month with her," she lied. "I just want to be with her for a while. I'll go home with the knowledge she's in good hands. I can see Mr. Delacourte is making every effort to learn how to care for her." *Until he tires of the novelty and hands her over to a new nanny in a long line of nannies!* she added mentally. "Please don't give me away! Once the month is over, I'll quietly disappear."

Goodberry pulled a handkerchief from his breast pocket, dabbed at his eyes, then covered his nose, blowing discreetly. She'd been right. He was a sentimental old darling. Hope surged in her breast.

As he stuffed the kerchief into his hip pocket, he seemed to gather himself together. "My dear," he said, his voice unsteady. "I see how your being mistaken for the nanny was a stroke of luck, considering all you'd been through." He straightened his shoulders; his expression remained troubled. "I don't keep things from Mr. Delacourte. He is my employer. I owe him my first loyalty."

Lauren experienced a sinking despair.

"However, in this case," he went on, "I can't see the harm in allowing you to spend time with Tina. After all, we're fairly remote. It's not like you could merely hail a cab."

Lauren heard it and her breath froze in her lungs.

He shook his head; a small, sad smile curved his

lips. "I will keep your secret, Lauren...rather Quinn. However—" his expression went solemn, his eyes flashing a caution "—I feel it only fair to warn you, I shall keep a keen eye on you. It's not that I don't believe you. It is true, I know your name, and for you to successfully steal the child would be all but impossible. Considering Mr. Delacourte's vast financial circumstances, you would be hard-pressed to hide anywhere in the world—for long."

She nodded. That was true, and one of the reasons she needed to win Tina legally. "I accept your offer, Goodberry." She took his hands in hers, squeezing. "Thank you so much for being understanding." She smiled, this time with real gratitude.

"Well, I'd best get on with the laundry." He touched her face, sweeping away a tear. "Don't worry, dear. Your secret is safe with me." A minute later, he was gone.

Deep down, Lauren felt like a snake, lying to the sweet man. But she couldn't dwell on that. Dade Delacourte was a bigger snake, with a whole lot more experience slithering on his belly! Besides wasn't the end worth *any* means, if it meant she could legally get custody of her niece?

Somewhere out there, Millie had disappeared back into the Hollywood scene, using a stage name in her quest to become a star. Lauren essentially had no family. Only Tina. She couldn't allow her dear niece to slip through her fingers.

Snagging Goodberry's silence was a major coup. Now she *knew* she wouldn't fail. All that was left was for Dade Delacourte to host one simple Chase Me Naked On The Beach party, and Lauren would have her evidence!

CHAPTER SEVEN

DADE was restless. His guests were due around four o'clock. For some reason he could barely stand the wait. He needed to be surrounded by familiar people, easy conversation, things he could control. So, here he was, in the front yard at one o'clock, playing Toss the Stick with Spikey. The dog snagged the chunk of wood in midair with a jaunty body flip, and Dade burst out laughing. "Good one, boy! Maybe I'll get a Frisbee and turn you into a champion."

Spikey pranced up to his master, tail wagging, as though he planned to present his trophy to him. When Dade grabbed the stick, Spikey segued into a vigorous version of his Growling And Tugging game. Dade was familiar with the mutt's penchant for the sport, and held on. "If you want me to toss it to you, old man, this is counterproductive."

Spikey didn't appear too concerned. He growled and yanked on Dade's hold.

"If I let go you're going to keel over on your fuzzy patoot."

Spikey snarled and jerked and strained and growled, his tail wagging as he dug in with his paws.

Dade grinned at the dog. "Spikey, when you're like this you remind me of Quinn. She's the most stubborn, rigid woman I've ever met. I'd like to see her wag her tail—just once."

Spikey let go and barked. The timing was so perfect, Dade had a feeling he'd just been chastised for making such a risqué suggestion about an employee.

"Hey, it was a joke," Dade muttered, hefting the stick and tossing it toward the side of the house. "Can't anybody take a joke around here?" As the dog spun away to chase the stick, Dade caught sight of movement in the distance, and realized the tail to which he'd referred was being presented to him right now. His nanny bent to pick a flower. From his perspective, she was around four inches tall, so she hadn't been close enough to hear him.

He watched her straighten and add the bright yellow flower to the colorful bouquet in her left hand. Tina rode in a carrier on Quinn's back, flapping little hands and legs, most likely squealing at the breeze or the dune grasses or the surf. He was a little sorry he couldn't hear her from the knoll where he stood.

He did hear something, however, and turned. The mail truck rumbled down his private road toward him so he waved. The postal worker was obliging, bringing his mail to the house instead of leaving it in the box beside the highway. Because of his extra consideration, Dade made sure he was compensated with a hefty Christmas check every year.

"Hello, Mr. Delacourte," the postman called out.

Dade walked to the driveway. "Hi, Al. Anything exciting?"

Al's truck crunched to a stop on the crushed shells, and the driver held out a stack of letters. "The regular. Two or three You've Already Won notices, a couple of Urgent! come-ons and the usual bills." He paused. "And a letter forwarded from your place in town."

Dade took it, noting it was from the agency that

sent him his nanny. With a curious frown, he looked it over. "Thanks, Al."

"See you tomorrow, Mr. Delacourte."

Dade nodded absently as he tore open the envelope. It was probably an advertisement or a questionnaire asking if the Delacourte family was satisfied with Quinn's services. He yanked out the letter, then felt something sharp and slimy rub against his leg. Glancing down, he noticed Spikey, poking his calf with the stick. "Okay, boy." He took the stick. The dog easily let go, possibly sensing his master was preoccupied. Dade gave the stick an inattentive toss. He unfolded the letter and scanned it, his frown deepening. Baffled, he read it again.

Dear Mr. Delacourte,

We at Manhattan Preferred Nannies have only today discovered that Madeline Quinn defaulted on her contract of employment with you. Had we been informed that she never arrived, we would have immediately located a replacement caregiver for you. Since we did not hear from you, I must presume you were too upset with us to offer MPN another opportunity to serve you.

We are extremely regretful of this appalling deviation from our normal quality service. This type of problem is rare at Manhattan Nannies, and we hope that in the future you give us another chance to assist you. I personally guarantee your satisfaction.

Yours most humbly and apologetically,

Gladys Gold, President

"Never arrived?" he mumbled. "But..." He looked up to scan the beach. She was right there, his niece strapped to her back. "Never arrived?" Of course she'd arrived. She'd been late, but she'd arrived. What was the idiotic Gladys Gold prattling about?

He headed toward the front door, needing to get to the bottom of this. Spikey beat him to the porch and barked as though demanding his master not go inside.

"Sorry, boy." He stooped to pat the dog's head. He went in, Spikey at his heels. Halfway to his den, he met Goodberry.

"Is something wrong, sir?"

Dade shook his head, then thought better of it and faced his manservant. Goodberry had been with the family too long not to know Dade's moods. "Look!" He thrust out the letter. "What kind of foolishness is this?"

Goodberry scanned the page. As Dade watched, the servant's complexion paled several shades. "Oh..." He didn't appear shocked, but looked more like he'd been caught with his hand in the cookie jar.

Dade plucked the letter from Goodberry's fingers, dark foreboding hardening in his gut. "You know something about this," he said.

True to the older gentleman's professionalism, he regained his aplomb. "Certain information has come to my attention, yes."

"Certain information?" Dade asked. "Like what?"

"Well—sir. Yesterday, I discovered Quinn is, in actuality, the child's aunt."

"The child's..." Dade's foreboding mutated into angry disbelief. "That woman is Tina's aunt? Her *blood* aunt?"

"Yes, sir."

"And you didn't tell me?" Dade felt extraordinarily betrayed. "What possible excuse could you have?"

"I confronted her, sir," Goodberry said quietly. "She explained she only recently found out where the baby was. She came to New York to make sure the child was being well cared for."

"Like hell!"

Goodberry straightened his shoulders, looking very dignified. His expression lacked any sign of intimidation. "Excuse me, sir, but when she was rushed up to your penthouse apartment, did you give her a chance to explain herself? Didn't you instead bellow at her and march her to the baby's room, demanding she prepare the child for the trip?"

"Well—naturally I assumed she was the nanny," Dade said, annoyed by Goodberry's exceptional memory. "I didn't bind and gag the woman!"

"You can be very intimidating, sir."

"I can see *that* by the way you grovel and whimper."

Goodberry's smile was compassionate. "I grovel and whimper inside, sir."

Dade snorted contemptuously. "How reassuring—and *don't* change the subject! Why didn't you tell me the minute you found out who she was? You must know she's here to steal Tina. What other reason could she have?"

"If I may continue—she told me when she was given the opportunity not only to see Tina, but spend time with her, she couldn't believe her luck. She'd worried about the baby for months. You see, her sister, Millie—Tina's mother—wanted revenge for the pregnancy and the—ahem—abandonment.''

Dade was aware of the careful way Goodberry referred to Joel's abominable behavior. Though Dade never told his servant that Joel was Tina's father, Goodberry knew both of the twins well. They were like sons to him. He also knew Dade had been in a remote area of Oregon, fishing, at the time the baby was conceived. However, since Dade took responsibility for Tina, Goodberry never mentioned Joel's name or any possible connection his reckless lifestyle might have to the birth. Unless Dade asked him to, the old gentleman would take his secret knowledge with him to his grave.

Goodberry went on. ''Millie ran away from Quinn's care just before the baby was due. Quinn knew Millie had no interest in her child. Her plan was to do to the father what he had done to her—force him to take responsibility for Tina, then Millie would vanish. Leaving—you—alone, with a baby to raise. According to Quinn, Tina's mother has probably returned to California, looking for fame and fortune in the movies.''

Goodberry shook his head. ''When Quinn was mistaken for the nanny, she took the opportunity to be with her niece for a while. Just a while, sir. That's all she asks.''

The servant's brow wrinkled, the only hint to his sensitive nature. ''I have a sixth sense about people, sir. She won't attempt to steal Tina. If you think about it, it's really very poignant, sir.''

''Poignant!'' Dade spat the word scornfully. ''It's bull! Don't be a fool, Goodberry. At her first chance, that woman is going to kidnap Tina.''

"With all due respect, sir. She won't do that."

"Are you implying you're psychic, now?" Dade was amazed by his outrage. After all, he didn't want Tina. An odd twinge in his chest made him flinch. *Did he?* Had his feelings altered in the months since his niece was thrust into his care?

His decision to accept responsibility had been out of obligation, not fondness. A flash of awareness hit like a boot in the gut. Good Lord, had his feelings for Tina grown deeper? In that instant, he grasped the truth—the quality of his life would *suffer* if his niece were taken from him.

"Please don't confront her, sir," Goodberry said, breaking through his thoughts. "Let her have her three weeks. All she wants is reassurance. All she asks is a little time."

"You're a sentimental boob, Goodberry."

"What would it hurt to wait a little, sir? Let her prove she's harmless by her actions?"

Dade was far from convinced the woman was harmless, but for some reason he vacillated about challenging Quinn.

Quinn!

"What's her real name?" he asked.

"Lauren, sir. Lauren Smith."

"Lauren..." As he spoke her name aloud, a chill went through him, making her deception all too real. Why did he feel so wounded over the fact that a woman he'd known less than a week had duped him. *Because, jackass, she's pretty, if somewhat prim, and you didn't give a thought to the possibility that underneath that innocent facade lurked a liar,* he charged mentally. *Because in your supreme arro-*

gance you were amused—and yes, attracted—by her earnest demeanor and charming naiveté.

Charming naiveté, *ha!* Exactly who had been the fox and who the self-satisfied rooster perched trustingly in his coop? "So, Tina is even named after her," he muttered.

"It seems so."

Damnation! The depth of his hurt and disappointment told him he'd grown fond of "Quinn" in the short time he'd known her. He'd found himself looking forward each evening to her piano playing and singing. Could he believe she was what she'd told Goodberry, or was she a skunk in the woodpile? Why was he even considering giving her the benefit of the doubt?

"I think I've come up with a way we can both keep our eyes on her, sir."

Dade snapped his attention to Goodberry. "You assume a great deal—I haven't decided to let her stay."

"Yes, you have, sir." The man affectionately touched his employer's arm. "You sense the same thing. She's a good person. And if you'll recall, the reason she's here is as much your doing as hers."

Dade ground his teeth, glowering at his manservant. The old scalawag had a point. A very *small* one—but undeniable. "What's your idea?" he asked, irritated with himself for behaving so illogically. What was it about the woman—

"You have no bed, sir. But the nursery has a cot. If you sleep there, you could be sure she didn't bolt with the child in the night."

Thunderstruck, he stared at Goodberry. "Lord, man, are you suggesting, I *sleep* with the nanny?"

"You have no bed, sir," Goodberry repeated calmly. "You want to keep an eye on Lauren—Quinn. Isn't that true?"

Dade heard a crackling sound and glanced down. He'd wadded the letter in his fist. He glared at Goodberry. "You burned my bed so I couldn't sleep with my girlfriend. Now you expect me to allow a conniving woman to stay in my employ—and that I *sleep* with her."

"The nursery cot is not exactly sleeping with her, sir."

"Don't be so blasted reasonable, man! Besides, there's Allegra to consider." He pinched the bridge of his nose to ward off a headache that had begun to throb behind his eyes. "Be honest with me, old boy, there is no such thing as fabric-eating mites."

Goodberry tsk-tsked, and when Dade eyed him again, the elderly servant smiled benignly. "Mr. Delacourte, sir, your lack of trust offends me."

"Oh, yes! And *why* exactly is it going to take three weeks to get me another bed?"

"I order your mattresses from Sweden, sir. For your bad back."

"I don't have a bad back!"

"Naturally, because I order your beds from—"

"Don't even say it!"

"Certainly, sir," Goodberry said. "On the former subject, Miss Allegra can use the twin bed in Mrs. Green's room. Mr. Green is unhappily unable to come."

"Allegra's going to freak!"

"If you say so, sir."

Dade eyed his servant, so annoyed he could hardly speak. "Give me one good reason why I should do this. I could get another nanny out here in two hours, and at the same time be rid of a potential kidnapper."

Why was he even discussing allowing the impostor to remain in contact with Tina? Perhaps because in one corner of his brain, a troublesome thought nagged. *If what Goodberry says is true, Lauren Smith's sister abandoned her baby to your care out of some twisted idea of vengeance. Then she ran off, concerned about nothing and nobody but herself. Ironically, then, Lauren's situation isn't so different from your own. She's a victim in all this, too.*

"I've given you all my reasons, sir," Goodberry stated softly. "Now, it's up to you."

Dade eyed heaven. *Give her time with the baby,* the voice in his head admonished. *She only wants to make sure Tina is okay. She knows you hold all the legal cards. You are Joel's identical twin. Even a DNA test would fail to prove you aren't Tina's father.*

That damnable inner voice hammered at his brain, driving him nuts. He scowled at his servant. "All right, Goodberry. I'll give our little fake nanny all the rope she needs to hang herself." His voice low and harsh, he added, "And I won't let her out of my sight."

Lauren took off her sandals and strolled through the frothy surf, enjoying the cool caress of the water. Or at least trying to enjoy it. She knew she was stalling and dawdling, not looking forward to getting back to the house—and the deception. Out here she could be herself, Aunt Lauren, and Tina could be her niece. There was no "nanny and her charge" out here. As she meandered along, Tina gab-gabbed pleasantly, chatting with seagulls and air and water, as though she were presiding over a board meeting or reciting Shakespeare on a stage.

Lauren smiled, but not without a melancholy tug at her heart. Tina came by her orating tendencies naturally—with an extrovert, wanna-be actress for a mother, and a masterly, captain of industry for a daddy.

She wished so much that Tina was really hers, that she could walk and walk along this beach until she ran into a town. Then she could make her way back to Oklahoma and settle in with her baby and get on with her life.

She scanned Dade's house, high on the bluff, amazed that it could look so grand and yet cozy at the same time. She liked its homey feel, its rustic warmth and breathtaking openness. She had enjoyed brightening it with flowers these past few days, and she'd especially loved playing his splendid piano.

She'd surprised herself several times, discovering she was humming as she went about her work. *Humming!* She didn't hum. Nevertheless, as she fed Tina or changed her or sat in the shade feeding her a bottle, she found herself humming more often than not. She'd even been embarrassed to notice Dade lolling in a doorway, listening, with that taunting little half smile riding his lips.

She wanted to shout, "So what if I hum! It isn't against the law for a nanny to hum! Go ahead and laugh for all I care!" But she prudently kept her mouth shut and her temper at bay. She had a mission, and all the smirks in the world were not going to derail her!

She pulled her glance from the house, trying to banish thoughts of Dade and his dimpled grin. She made herself look out to sea, to inhale the tangy breeze. She tried to concentrate on the scenery, on the pleasant feel of wet sand as it oozed between her toes, of Tina as she gaily babbled and cooed.

Drat Dade and his charisma. She refused to allow herself to believe he could lure her into his web as effortlessly as he'd seduced Millie. Lauren had always prided herself as being levelheaded, not prone to flights of fancy about men or anything else. So why, then, did the sound of his laughter make her pulse race, or his nonchalant touch send her wits into a spin? She wanted to loathe the man. *Needed to.*

Resolve hardened her heart.

This weekend would surely give her proof of Dade's depravity. Still, knowing this—*wanting* this—a wayward part of her mourned the fact that he had a steady woman friend with whom he would be sleeping.

Wild, wicked visions raced before her mind's eye. She groaned, striving to squelch them. The last thing she wanted was to think about Dade and Allegra on the moonlit beach, writhing naked, panting and moaning!

She bit her lip hard, furious with herself. *Great, Lauren, you're doing a fine job of keeping your mind on the scenery! Except the scenery does not consist of intertwined nude bodies—at least not for a few more hours!*

The guests arrived while Tina napped. Lauren opted to stay in their two-room suite, straightening this and that. Mainly she was hiding, trying to stay out of sight while the lecherous throngs poured into the house and got settled. For some reason, she especially didn't want to meet Allegra. She didn't know why. Heavenly days, she knew how things were in these permissive times. Marriage wasn't necessary in relationships. Lauren simply had no desire to meet the female half of Dade's current sexual partnership until she had to. If at all.

Lauren figured, as the nanny, she wouldn't be in demand this weekend, anyway. She was sure the less her boss had to deal with his bothersome baby while he had guests, the better.

She rocked Tina before her sliding glass door, feeding the baby her afternoon bottle. In the quiet, she watched the surf roll peacefully to shore, incessantly, everlastingly. Each time the waves advanced, skimmed over the sand, then retreated out to sea, was as fascinating and soothing as the time before.

After a while, Lauren heard lighthearted chitchat, and guessed the partyers had migrated to the patio. Tina had just emptied her bottle, so Lauren burped her and lay her on a blanket with her favorite toys. Against her better judgment, she returned to the window and peeked in the direction of the Great Room where the main expanse of redwood deck stretched out toward the ocean.

A leggy blonde walked to the railing and gazed toward the sea. Her long, straight hair was almost platinum, and fluttered in the breeze like those shampoo ad models. She wore a short pink T-shirt that showed off a slender midriff. Her shorts were a bright rose, as were her platform sandals. "Allegra," she muttered, then pulled her lips between her teeth, chagrined that she'd spoken aloud.

"No, it's me."

Startled to hear Dade's voice, she spun around. He

stood in the open door looking casually gorgeous in beige shorts and a matching polo. His hair was just windswept enough to be painfully sexy. "I didn't mean to scare you—Quinn." He watched her oddly, not quite smiling but not frowning. He seemed to scrutinize her. It was almost as though he was seeing her for the first time. "I'd like you to bring Tina out to meet the guests. And I want them to meet you, too, of course."

She was stunned by his request. "Oh—when?"

"Whenever. Dinner won't be until eight. Several of us are going swimming. Ingrid Green doesn't swim so she won't go, and Hadley Wayland won't, either. I guess that leaves me, Allegra and Joyce who'll be swimming. Anyway, Ingrid is dying to see the baby."

Joyce and Allegra and Dade will be swimming, she mused. *How cozy!*

"As soon—" Her voice was unusually shrill. She cut off her remark and cleared her throat. "As soon as I change, I'll take Tina out on the deck."

"Change?" He surveyed her green shift. "You look fine to me. Unless you have shorts. We'll all be pretty casual this weekend. You might as well be, too."

She stared. "Shorts?"

A brow rose. "Sure. Or does Dr. Wickerfurniture think it would be too much pressure on a female baby?"

"Pressure?" Lauren was confused.

"To see attractive adult female legs at such a tender age."

That sounded like a compliment. Or was he being sarcastic? "I—I don't..."

He grinned, or at least half grinned. ‘‘Never mind, Quinn. Did you bring any shorts?’’

‘‘No, sir.’’

‘‘No, Dade,’’ he corrected. ‘‘I’ll see what Goodberry can scrounge up for tomorrow. Tonight, you’re fine.’’

She nodded, still not clear on what he expected of her. ‘‘I’m glad.’’

He chuckled. ‘‘Yeah, you look glad.’’

Her cheeks heated at his teasing. ‘‘Are you suggesting you want me to join the party?’’

He lounged against the doorjamb. ‘‘Is that a problem?’’

Of course it’s a problem! she shot back telepathically. *I do not intend for Tina to witness naked volleyball on the beach!* ‘‘I’m not much of a party girl.’’ She thought fast, needing to come up with a foolproof excuse. ‘‘I don’t think Tina’s schedule…’’

‘‘We won’t keep her up till all hours playing poker,’’ he said, still grinning that crooked grin. ‘‘She can go to bed whenever you say. How’s that?’’

Lauren chewed the inside of her cheek. Grasping at straws, she said, ‘‘There’s a school of thought that states, children—’’

‘‘The baby book I read says infants benefit from a certain amount of socialization, as long as it’s monitored and not overdone. I’ll leave the monitoring to you. Okay?’’

Drat the man, flaunting his knowledge of The Book! Why, oh why, couldn’t she have had the chance to get through it? Reluctantly she nodded. ‘‘All right. But, I insist on having the last word, si—Dade.’’

‘‘Fine.’’ He walked toward her, and for some idiotic reason she found it necessary to plaster herself against the cool glass. What did she think he was going to do, pounce on her? What a silly idea. Just because he looked at her a little peculiarly...

"By the way, I thought you ought to know." When he reached the blanket where his niece lay, he knelt and extended a finger. Tina promptly grabbed it, squealing with delight.

"What did you think I should know?" she asked, a little breathless. Did he want to be sure she was aware of the twistedness of things to come—warn her that after ten o'clock clothes were optional? Was he about to tell her that if she didn't want to be horrified by the goings-on she'd better lock herself in the safety of her suite?

He glanced her way. When their gazes met, she noticed he'd lowered his lids to half-mast. He could see out but she couldn't see in. "I'll be sleeping in the nursery," he said. "I trust that won't be a problem."

CHAPTER EIGHT

DADE watched Lauren as she absorbed the news that he would be sleeping in a bed not fifteen feet away from hers—in a room without a door to separate them. She didn't look well. He postulated there was more to her pallor than a fear of lost modesty. Her plan to sneak out some dark night with Tina would be badly compromised with *him* in the baby's room. When she didn't respond, he decided he'd better go on. He needed to have her agree, and by the look of things she was not only going to disagree, but she was going to faint.

"As you know, I have no bed," he said as nonchalantly as he could. "As you may not know, Goodberry has a badly deviated septum, and snores like a revving jet engine. No human being with normal hearing should be condemned to such a fate." He tried on a smile to see if she would reciprocate.

Nothing. Pallid skin and wide, incredulous eyes were his only answer.

"Allegra will bunk in with Ingrid Green," he went on, keeping his voice casual, though the memory of Allegra's reaction to the arrangement made him want to wince. She was *not* happy, though she was putting on an untroubled front. "That only leaves the cot in the nursery." He shoved Allegra's anger to the back of his mind and smiled. It was the most reassuring grin in his arsenal, the one he reserved for daughters of employees on Mothers and Daughters Day, when working moms brought their little girls to work. "I promise to be a gentleman, Miss Quinn. I know this is an intrusion, but I wouldn't think of trespassing on your privacy."

She blinked, a bright pink spot of color surfacing high on each cheek. "Uh," she began, her voice high-pitched. She stopped, swallowed. "Couldn't you move the cot—elsewhere?"

He was ready for that argument. "I've heard babies don't take nights off. If I'm to learn to care for Tina properly, I must be proficient at night duty, too. You don't want me to be derelict in my fatherly duties, do you?"

Her face fairly glowed. He watched her grit her teeth. She didn't like this one bit. *Well, join the club, sweetheart!*

He waited, but she didn't speak. "It's an inconvenience for me, too, Miss Quinn," he said. Shrugging, he refreshed his grin, trying to appear harmless, a man without secret agendas. "Let's agree to make the best of it." He held out a hand.

He felt like a political candidate electioneering in his opposition's stronghold, standing there forcing a smile, his hand thrust forward. But *blast it,* he would *not* leave the room until he had her well in line.

"Quinn?" he said quietly. "Are you there?"

She blinked, but otherwise didn't move.

"Shake?" He moved closer. Close enough to detect that unusual scent of honeysuckle and oranges. He had the fleeting thought again of his erotic dream almost a week ago—when that scent seemed to linger in the air. How bizarre.

Suddenly she literally shook herself out of her stupor. Clearly hesitant, she slid her hand into his. Her fingers were cold, her grip far from firm. "I—I suppose there's no choice?" she whispered. The way she phrased the question, it sounded like a plea for a heavenly reprieve.

"I'm afraid not." He squeezed her fingers. "Thank you for understanding."

She hurriedly withdrew her hand. "I—I'd better see to Tina—get her changed."

He stuck his hands into his pockets and nodded. "Right. And I have a date to go swimming." He noticed she plunged her hands into her pockets, too. They stood there for a minute, watching each other in the silence. He wanted badly to know what thoughts ran through her head. When he realized his "trust me" smile had vanished, he pulled himself together. "I'd better go." He flashed his fake grin. "I'll have Goodberry bring down some of my things later."

She nodded.

"I'll tell him to check into what we have in the way of women's casual clothes for you."

Dade wouldn't have believed it possible, but the glow in her cheeks actually deepened. He scanned her flushed face. Her lips were slightly parted, her shimmering eyes, wide with panic. She might be a conniver and a liar, but she blushed better than any woman he knew. His lips twitched rebelliously in appreciation. Obviously she hadn't expected to be included in the party, and had no desire to be. Well, that was just too bad. He didn't intend to leave her to her own devices, not with Tina in her care. "Do you like to swim, Quinn?" he asked quietly.

She swallowed. "I don't think my duties will allow—"

"Why don't we play it by ear?" He turned away, effectively cutting off any argument. He intended to have his deceitful little nanny within view every feasible moment. "I'll leave you to get Tina ready."

By the time he closed the door between them, she hadn't uttered another word. Out in the hallway, he switched off his smile. "*Now* try to take Tina away from me, Miss Smith," he muttered. "Just try."

Lauren frittered away a lot of extra time changing Tina. She finally decided she'd put it off long enough and dressed the baby in a pink playsuit with a little bunny embroidered on the front. She slipped on pink booties and tied the ribbons so Tina would have a hard time kicking them off. She even spent several enjoyable minutes brushing the fine, blond hair into a little curl on the top of the baby's head. "You look darling, sweetie," she whispered, kissing Tina on her rosy cheek. "If we have to go out there, we might as well wow 'em."

Lauren had no idea what to expect from Dade's guests. She'd seen Allegra, the leggy beauty, but she hadn't had a glimpse of the rest of them. So when she stepped out onto the deck, she was startled to see a stout woman in her mid-forties and a man of about the same age, his right leg in a cast.

At the sound of the door, both seated guests turned. The woman's Pekingese face lit up. "Oh, the darling baby!" She held out her hands. "Give me that sweet child!" She had long carrot red hair, done in one thick braid. Tossing it back over her shoulder she smiled at Lauren. "You're Quinn? I'm Ingrid Green." The older woman shifted in her chair to get a better look at them.

While Ingrid looked, so did Lauren. The seated woman wore an oversize plaid shirt and loose jeans. Not the sexy attire Lauren expected. But who knew what wild thoughts lurked in that carrot-topped head?

"Dade has praised you to the skies, dear," the woman said. "He neglected to mention how pretty you are. I expected a wizened old granny type." She wagged her fingers. "Now give me that baby, immediately. Don't worry, I have two sweet grandbabies of my own. They live in Seattle, so I don't get to see them nearly enough."

Lauren liked the woman and was startled to feel that way. Without hesitation she handed Tina over. If anybody loved babies, Lauren could tell this woman did. "You said your name is Ingrid?" Lauren asked.

"Yes, dear," she said, cuddling Tina to her breast. "I was Dade's secretary until my husband, Humphrey, decided to retire. He said we'd travel. But as it turns out, he plays golf every waking minute. The most traveling I've done so far is to the mailbox for his postcards." She offered Tina a finger and the baby took it. "Hump made the finals in some silly old-duffer tournament in Indiana this weekend, so he couldn't make it." She sighed and goo-gooed at Tina. "I see him less now than I did when he was working." With a light laugh she shook her head, glancing at Lauren. "I should never have quit my job with Dade. It was great money and he was the perfect boss." She turned toward the beach. "Speaking of Dade, it looks like they're through with their swim."

Lauren didn't want to look, but her eyes disobeyed her command to remain on Ingrid. She saw him, tall, broad shouldered, his tan muscles shiny in the sun. She watched him stroll hand in hand with the two women, wondering what "the perfect boss" comment meant. She eyed him as he walked toward the house with his two female companions. Lauren heard throaty laughter, and instinctively knew it came from Allegra.

"I'm Hadley Wayland."

Lauren dragged her attention from the trio on the beach to the man who had spoken. Sword-thin, in his late forties, Hadley Wayland had a thick crop of brown hair, salted with gray, and a prominent aristocratic nose. His smile was broad and friendly. When he held out a hand, she took it. "How do you do, Mr. Wayland."

"Call me Hadley." He indicated the seashore with a nod. "The shorter woman out there is Joyce, my better half."

Lauren examined Joyce. Short, thick-waisted and slightly bowlegged, she didn't look the party type. She looked more like a Scout leader; a sturdy, birdhouse-building type. Lauren supposed just because she looked wholesome didn't mean she was.

Allegra, on the other hand, looked anything but wholesome. Even wet, her blond hair wagged in the breeze like a sexy come-on. And in that skimpy, white two-piece bathing suit, hardly a detail of her willowy ripeness was hidden from view. With her narrow waist and zeppelinlike breasts, she was the essence of the term "mantrap." For some shapeless reason, Lauren felt a little sick to her stomach.

"I'm Dade's senior VP," Hadley went on, drawing her back. He indicated his leg. "As you can see I'm not vice president of Impeccable Walking." He released her hand and slapped his cast. "I did this tripping on my own shoelace."

Ingrid tittered. "Don't believe it, Miss Quinn. Hadley's so smart, his brain's just too heavy, and he keeps toppling over." She made a face at the man. "Don't blame your poor shoes, dear."

Hadley guffawed, and Lauren found herself smiling. Both Ingrid and Hadley seemed genuinely nice—on the surface. Nothing like the sleek, wild-eyed debauchees she'd expected.

"What's so funny?" Dade called from the stairs.

Lauren turned in time to see him appear as he mounted the steps. The two women were ahead of him. Joyce arrived on the deck first. She hurried to a nearby table that held fluffy white beach towels and wrapped herself up. "That was so refreshing! Hadley, it's such a shame you couldn't join us."

"Right, rub it in," Hadley said with a laugh.

Lauren watched Allegra sweep onto the deck. She didn't head for a towel. She merely lounged against the railing as if she was expecting to be photographed for the *Sports Illustrated* swimsuit edition cover. Sweeping a hand through her hair she smiled. Heavenly days! She was dazzling, with the prettiest green eyes. Like polished emeralds. Lauren had always wished her olive-drab eyes had been a brighter shade of green.

"It was wonderful!" She reached out to take Dade's hand as he joined her. "I've always said, this is the loveliest place in the world to swim."

Dade's deep laugh filled the air. "I've never heard you say that."

She clutched his arm against her breast and tilted her chin in the most flagrantly coquettish way. "Maybe you haven't been listening, darling."

He gave her a look, his grin crooked. One brow

rose. Lauren didn't want to think about what silent message he was sending. Something like, *Meet me on the beach at midnight, my little enchantress, and I'll do much, much more than listen!*

My little enchantress, indeed! Lauren tore her stare from the couple and focused on Tina. Ingrid tickled the baby's cheek and goo-gooed at her. Tina gurgled and grinned. Lauren managed a real smile. Yes, this was what she must concentrate on. Her niece—her purity and sweet innocence. Not Dade and his gushy nymph.

A disruptive sound drew everybody's attention to the open patio doors in time to witness Goodberry lurch onto the deck. His usual dignity had deserted him, but not his grin, which was thoroughly impish. Right behind him came Braga, screeching in Portuguese and waving a ladle like a club. The language barrier was no obstacle to grasping her intentions. The woman was bent on bashing the grinning Gentleman's Gentleman on the head.

Goodberry galloped around the deck, doing one complete circle before he escaped inside, Braga hot on his heels. Lauren stared in awe. Though she'd seen this fascinating spectacle a time or two before, she still couldn't quite believe it.

Dade's laughter was a rich, deep roar. "I believe dinner may be a few minutes late." He faced his guests. "That should give Allegra, Joyce and me time to change into something dryer." His glance fell on Lauren, and she thought she saw a slight narrowing of his eyes. "Ah, our nanny and Tina have joined us." He lifted an arm in her direction. "Everybody, meet Quinn. Quinn, I presume you've already been introduced to Ingrid and Hadley?"

She nodded. "Yes—Dade."

"Good." He took Allegra's hand and waved toward Joyce, who had taken a chair next to her husband. "This is Allegra Brooks and the lovely woman in the towel is Joyce Wayland."

Lauren smiled at them as they were introduced to her. "How do you do?"

Allegra gave Quinn a strange look, a tiny frown forming on her forehead. She whispered something to Dade, but kept her eyes on Lauren. Dade shook his head and laughed. Lauren had a feeling Allegra asked if Dade was really sleeping with the nanny rather than the baby.

"Hi, Quinn," Joyce said, drawing Lauren's attention. "As soon as I get changed, I'm going to take my turn with that darling baby. Ingrid, don't get too attached. You have to share, girl."

"You see, Quinn," Dade said, "Tina will benefit from a little socializing and you'll get a break."

"I don't need a break, sir—Dade," she said, not pleased with the way events were shaping up. What would a real nanny do? Would she put her foot down, insist Tina not be passed around like some—some basketball? Of course, two doting women weren't exactly the true definition of "passed around."

"Everyone needs a break, Quinn." Dade pushed away from the rail and moved toward her. Too much taut, tan flesh for comfort. Lauren turned away, but almost immediately felt his hand at her arm. "You'll join us for dinner, of course."

She faced him, startled. "But the baby."

"Oh, please let me feed her," Ingrid said. "This is such a cute age." She indicated her clothes. "As you can see, I'm dressed for the mess."

Lauren was taken aback. The mess? Was Ingrid saying all babies of this age made a mess of eating? That it might not be just her own ineptitude? "Well—I..."

"Since you're prepared for a mess, Ingrid, you're in for a wonderful time," Dade broke in, his dimpled grin doing unruly things to Lauren's insides.

"I can't wait!" Ingrid said. "It'll be like having my own darlings around."

Dade shifted to smile at Lauren, his eyes strangely veiled. "You see, Quinn, you have no excuse. Dinner will be in fifteen minutes."

Lauren didn't know whether to get into her nightshirt or not. No matter how much Dade insisted he wouldn't trespass on her privacy, he had to walk through her room to get to his—unless he crawled in the nursery window. She wished she'd insisted on that route when he'd first mentioned his intention to sleep in the nursery. But even if she hadn't been too shocked to speak, she supposed demanding the master of the house climb in through windows to get to his bed was a bit much.

Did it really matter? He'd probably be gone most of the night, anyway. Surely he and Allegra would seek out places to—to be together. On the beach, in the back seat of his limo, even on his bedroom floor. If she remembered correctly there was a thick rug at the foot of his bed. People made love on rugs—

A knock at her door brought her head up, and she jumped off the edge of her mattress. "Yes?"

"It's Dade."

She frowned in confusion, but walked to the door and opened it. "Yes?"

Looming there, haloed by a wall sconce, he looked unearthly, like a tall, powerfully built archangel. Though his face was in shadow, his teeth seemed to flash with his grin. "I thought I'd come to bed."

She stared, befuddled. "At eleven o'clock?" She'd only left the partyers fifteen minutes ago. Joyce had tucked Tina into bed at nine, and there hadn't been a peep out of the darling. So everybody had insisted she stay and play charades with them, to even out the teams.

Dade propped a shoulder against the wall, looking gorgeous and cuddly, his hair mussed charmingly by the night breeze. "I can't go to bed at eleven o'clock?" He crossed his arms before him, looking both amused and skeptical. "I don't recall that rule."

"I—I mean..." *What about your fun and games with Allegra? You haven't had time to get undressed, let alone...* She pursed her lips, scrambling around for words. "I thought you would, er, *visit* Allegra..." Her face sizzled. What craziness had prompted that remark?

His cheek muscles stood out when he clenched his jaw. "I'm not in the habit of discussing my personal life." He pushed away from the wall. "Granted, our situation is exceptional, so you may have more right to ask questions than most." He indicated her door with a nod. "But not about this. If you'll move aside, I'd like to go to bed."

She felt thoroughly dismissed. It might be her suite, but it was his house. Without another word, she stepped out of his way and allowed him to pass by.

"I sleep in a T-shirt," she called out, then bit her tongue. Why did she think it was necessary to blurt that?

He turned. "And you're telling me this because...?"

"Because..." It was a mystery to her, too. She improvised. "Because it's not exactly street attire. I'd prefer it if you keep that in mind before you start wandering around at night."

His brow wrinkled. "I'm not in the habit of wandering around at night."

"Okay, when you're going to or from the bathroom."

"Maybe you should heed your own warning, Quinn. The bath is in my room. And since you brought it up, I sleep in the buff."

She gasped. "No you *don't!*"

"I don't?"

Every inch of her body flamed. She knew he slept naked. She'd only been spared complete mortification the night she'd broken in on him by the fact that a sheet had covered the lower half of his body. "You *don't* sleep in the buff while you're bunking in the nursery. I have to go in there to check Tina from time to time."

"What do you expect me to do, sleep in a shirt and tie?"

"Don't be funny," she said. "A tie won't be necessary. I've seen your neck naked, and it's not that offensive.

"I'm flattered."

"Good for you." She made a disgruntled face. "I don't think that's too much to ask to *expect* you to be decent."

"What's your idea of decent?"

"Shorts."

"Will you be wearing shorts?" he asked, his expression wry.

"I told you I wear a T-shirt."

"How long is it?"

"Long enough."

He eyed her for a moment. "See that it is. I'm very sensitive about such things."

His lips twitched and she knew he was taunting her. "I suppose the sight of a woman's bare thigh gives you the hives?"

His grin was brief, but telling. "I'm laid up for weeks."

Exasperated, she smirked. "I'm not surprised. It's obvious by the way you act around women you're not comfortable with them." She couldn't help herself. The sly, womanizing fox! It was all his fault. If he didn't insist on goading her she wouldn't feel the need to get him back. "Maybe you should go to a counselor, try to find a way to relate to women—instead of being so painfully awkward around them."

"Awkward?" he echoed, sounding incredulous.

"I believe I said *painfully* awkward. My heart cries out in pity for you."

"It does?" His eyes twinkled in the reflected lamplight. "How kind. I don't think any woman has ever told me her heart cries out in pity for me, before."

"I find that hard to swallow." For some crazy reason she was enjoying their repartee. She couldn't imagine why he was allowing her to joke about his masculine prowess with women. She'd come to the conclusion he didn't take jokes about himself well. *Possibly this topic is acceptable,* an inner voice chided, *because, where women are concerned, Dade*

Delacourte is so utterly confident he finds your insinuation that he's inept hilarious.

Which, of course, it was. She'd been around him long enough to know the man didn't have an inept bone in his hunky body. *No! No, don't think hunky!*

"Did you say something?" he asked.

"I hope not," she muttered.

"It sounded like hunky."

Flustered that her mouth would betray her, she floundered. "Certainly not! Hunky's not even a word."

"Yes, it is. It's slang for—"

"I don't care what it's slang for! I didn't say it!"

"My mistake. What were we talking about?" He sat down on the wicker love seat. *What was he doing?* "Oh, yes," he continued, "You were saying something about finding it hard to swallow that no woman's heart has cried out in pity to me before. Right?" He stretched out long legs. The lamplight emphasized the hunch of thigh muscles as he relaxed. Lauren didn't know when she'd seen a more stirring sight. She forced her gaze away.

"Why are you sitting down?" Panic edged her voice. "I thought you wanted to go to bed."

He stretched, drawing her gaze to his face. "I'm getting my second wind. Want some coffee? I can ring Goodberry."

"No!" Her response was too harsh for the question he'd asked. But she couldn't help it. She didn't like this obliged confinement with him. Dade made her nervous, and—well—*nervous!* "I need to get to bed, Mr. Delacourte."

"Dade," he corrected with a slow grin that would charm the pants off the devil. He patted the love seat.

"Sit. I want to hear more about this pity you feel for me."

"I was *kidding!* Can't you tell when a person is kidding?"

"You, Quinn? Kidding? I thought you were the epitome of sobriety."

"After eleven o'clock, sometimes I kid."

He laced his fingers behind his head, looking her up and down. "Really? Now that's interesting."

"No, it's not."

"Tell me, Quinn. What do you do after midnight?" His eyes were skeptical and teasing and alluring.

She noticed she'd unconsciously drawn to within an inch of the love seat, and hurriedly backed up a couple of steps. Darn his magnetism. He dispersed it like cold germs. She was appalled at how much she wanted to—to—*sneeze!* Jabbing a finger toward the nursery entrance, she glared at him. "I believe your bed is in *there.* I need my sleep."

"You're kidding, right?"

"No, I'm *not* kidding!" she cried, aggravated to the point of strangling him.

He quirked a brow, looking perplexed, though she knew it was a lie. "But you said, after eleven you—"

She leaped at him, heaving a frustrated moan. "Up! *Get up!*" She grabbed his wrists and yanked, but he didn't budge.

"Why, Miss Quinn, I thought we'd made a pact about touching. And here you are, riding me like a little bronco buster."

Horrified, she let go and stumbled backward. What had she done? She'd had to straddle his thighs to grab his wrists. *Straddle his thighs!* Where had her mind gone? She clamped her teeth around a low, guttural moan.

"Apology accepted." He stood, eyeing her with a crooked grin. "Quinn, it seems there's more to you than first meets the eye." He turned toward the nursery, then stopped and glanced back. "I'm anxious to see what the next three weeks will reveal."

A heartbeat later, he disappeared into the darkness of Tina's room. Shaky, Lauren sank to the wicker settee. Her bones suddenly mush, she sagged back and closed her eyes.

"Oh, Quinn?"

She jerked up to sit stiffly and stared toward the nursery entrance. He was grinning, but the expression seemed more cynical than friendly.

"What?" she asked, almost too breathlessly to be heard.

He grasped the jamb above the door with both hands, his manner a lot more casual and relaxed than she felt. "I thought I'd better warn you. I'm going to take a shower."

She glowered at him. "Thanks. That *is* scary."

His chuckle was deep, warm and rich, and she tried hard to hate the sound of it.

CHAPTER NINE

LAUREN was becoming more and more confused as the weekend progressed—without a single wild party. Earlier that day, she'd been included in a picnic. *A picnic!* There had been no nudity—unless you counted Allegra's near-nothing bathing suit. Every time the blond bombshell wiggled by, Lauren had the urge to cover Tina's innocent little eyes. Otherwise, the afternoon had been a lot more wholesome than anything she'd imagined, with Dade playing Toss the Stick with Spikey and helping Joyce find interesting seashells. He even insisted on giving Tina her afternoon bottle!

Lauren spent quite a bit of time chatting with Hadley and Ingrid about innocuous, pleasant things, like the current bestselling thriller they'd all read or a particularly funny movie. Except for Allegra and her homicidal glances, Lauren decided she liked Dade's friends. This was bad. Where was all her proof Dade was an unfit father? When was he going to reveal his true, depraved character? It was a strange irony that Lauren could enjoy herself so thoroughly yet be so upset at the same time.

That evening, long after dinner, Hadley and Joyce had gone to bed. Dade and Allegra excused themselves, and Ingrid insisted she and Tina needed some one-on-one story time in the Great Room's comfortable rocking chair.

Left on her own, Lauren was restless, unable to

reconcile her conflicted feelings about the way things were going. She knew she wouldn't be able to sleep, so she decided to take a walk along the beach.

She had no idea where Dade and Allegra were, and didn't want to think about it. Dade's sex life was none of her business—except for the creation of her sweet niece.

Lauren didn't want to care what Dade and Allegra were up to, but she did, darn her contrary hide! Unfortunately it was beginning to look like Dade wasn't the rogue she'd believed him to be. This new twist confounded her. Was his dalliance with Millie a deviation from his normal behavior?

She'd spent a week in close contact with him, and she had to admit he didn't seem like the type to pick up waitresses and lie to them in order to get a quick tumble. Why had he bothered to tell Millie he could get her into movies? He could walk up to any woman and say, "*Hi, there.* You appeal to me. Let's have sex," and ninety-nine percent would smile agreeably and take his arm, no strings attached. He had *that* much charisma.

She cringed, recalling how she'd straddled him last night when she'd grabbed his arms! There had been no need to. No need at all, except she'd been so—

"Hi, there."

She spun at the sound of Dade's voice. "*No! I won't have sex with you!*" She spotted him the same instant she realized she'd said that out loud. Horror filled her soul.

Dade sat on the beach, alone. His legs were outstretched, his arms braced slightly behind him. His wet swimsuit left little of his marvelous body to the imagination.

At her blurted remark, his eyes widened and his grin turned wry. "I never knew 'Hi there' could be taken that way."

Humiliated, she muttered, "I—I misunderstood."

"I thought you and Tina had gone to bed."

"Ingrid wanted to rock her. I decided to give them some time alone. And I'm—not tired." Avoiding eye contact, Lauren scanned the area, assuming the beautiful Allegra would rise out of the water like some mythical ocean goddess. Moonlight made the undulating surface quite distinct. When she couldn't spot the blonde anywhere, she glanced at Dade. "Where's Allegra?"

He bent a knee and wrapped an arm around it, the simple move alarmingly sensual. "She had a headache." He peered into the distance. "The truth? She's punishing me for the sleeping arrangements." He glanced at her, his grin weary. "I could strangle Goodberry."

Charmed by his unexpected openness, she giggled.

He cocked his head, looking skeptical. "I'm happy I could brighten your day."

She waved a negating hand, but couldn't hide her grin. "No—I'm sorry. It's not funny. It's just that—"

"Walking on the beach makes you giddy?"

"Yes—that's it," she joked. In an attempt to regain her poise, she pursed her lips, but another wayward laugh escaped. "I get hysterical when I walk along beaches." His remark hadn't been that funny, so she decided stress was to blame.

He nodded, skepticism changing to amusement. "Maybe you'd better sit, then. Until the fit passes."

When he took her hand, the contact so startled her, she lurched away. That turned out to be a bad move.

She stumbled over his bent leg and fell in his lap. He grabbed her, saving her from the inelegant fate of sliding off and thudding to her back. Instead she found herself clutched breast to chest with him. When she opened her eyes, all she could see was his mouth. Very close to her own.

In the moonlight, his lips seemed fuller. They were slightly parted as though goading her to take one, small taste—just to satisfy her curiosity.

"Are you okay?" he whispered, sounding a little hoarse.

She nodded, her attention concentrated on his mouth, slyly provocative. She couldn't form words. While sprawled in his lap, her brain had gone numb. She gaped, helpless.

"I'm glad you're not hurt," he murmured.

His breath feathered her lips, and she felt a tingling pull at her insides. The sensation of his warm strength all around her, his breath on her mouth, constricted her breathing and made her heart rate double. A disobedient tremor of wanting ran through her. Impulsively she slid her arms around him.

His lips, so sensuously masculine, pulled down slightly at the corners, and he groaned deep in his throat. Lauren hardly had time to register the averse reaction before his mouth found hers, hard and hungry. Slipping a hand to her waist, he pulled her into him. His touch was firm, his kiss coaxing, urging.

Her lips parted in invitation, and he accepted. Their kiss deepened, inflaming her. The intimate contact they shared was bold and thrilling, yet something in his kiss spoke of tenderness, even vulnerability. This achingly sweet element was so unexpected—especially from a man Lauren thought to be without a heart—she was nearly undone. Never had she experienced a kiss that could excite and comfort, ignite and nourish, all at the same time.

Her body quivered with the solid feel of him, of his big hands on her. She burned with a desire to know him passionately—sexually!

Sexually!

The word ricocheted around in her brain. Sexually. She wanted Dade Delacourte to make wild, crazy love to her. She wanted to experience him the way Millie had! Crazy, rash Millie—

A painful catch in her breast made her recoil. *Millie—and Dade.* This was the man who had abandoned her sister, left her pregnant and alone! Goodness, what was she doing? What was she thinking? How could she cling to him, want him with all her heart and soul, knowing…knowing…

With a moan of self-disgust, she dragged her arms from around his chest and pushed. Hard. *"No!"* she protested, her voice a feeble cry. She lunged to the sand. Her body insubstantial, she struggled to right herself.

"Damn!" he muttered. Somehow his anger gave her the strength she needed to rise to her feet and run.

His curse echoed in her ears as she fled. Obviously Allegra's rejection had been to blame for his unrestraint. He was primed and ready and sexually frustrated when his clumsy nanny fell in his lap. *And wrapped her foolish arms around him!* She'd practically compelled him into kissing her!

"Congratulations, Lauren," she muttered, stumbling away. "You now have absolute proof—of your own *stupidity!*"

* * *

The night was too chilly for sleeping on the beach in nothing but wet trunks. He'd needed a cold swim after Allegra's spiteful rebuff, but he hadn't needed a lapful of Lauren Smith! Or her kiss, either. What had possessed him? Not only was she his employee, but she was the sneak with plans to steal his Tina!

He stood up. *Blast!* It was ridiculous to sit in the sand all night when he had a perfectly comfortable bed to go to. He exhaled heavily. Well, maybe it wasn't that comfortable, but it was more comfortable than this. "Women," he muttered. First Allegra, thinking holding herself from him was going to be such a huge punishment. It was irritating, but he'd live. He'd come to realize this weekend she had no interest whatsoever in children.

It was odd how his priorities had changed since Tina had come into his life. Seven months ago, if he'd met a women with an interest in children, he would have run for the nearest exit. He chuckled at the irony. Now when he looked at a woman, the first question that came to mind was, "What kind of mother would she make?"

Maybe it was just as well Allegra had decided to punish him. Whatever relationship they'd had was over. He had a child to think about, and he didn't intend to have her snubbed and ignored and looked upon like some detestable pet reptile, the way Allegra had done all weekend.

He bounded up the steps to the patio and started for the Great Room when he noticed movement off to his right. He stopped and stared into the shadows. He saw it again. The flutter of a sheer curtain. Lauren's sliding door was open.

He walked toward it, deciding that would be the

quickest way to his room. He had to go past Lauren's bed either way. He peered in, startled to see his fraudulent nanny asleep in the rocker, just inside the open door. She wore a long T-shirt that exposed her knees and a few inches of thigh. Her hands were curled loosely in her lap.

Her head lolled almost to one shoulder. Her hair, which she usually wore clipped in a swirl at her nape, was loose and fell around her face. Light wisps quivered with the breeze. He frowned at her, his gaze sliding to her lips. The memory of the kiss they shared loomed in his mind. Of her beautiful breathless urgency. The hungry, eager way she'd clung to him. The tiny sound of wonder that escaped her throat. He experienced a tightening coil in his gut, and raked a hand through his hair.

He didn't like being so aware of her whenever she entered a room, or so disturbed when she left. He didn't want to be enticed by her honeysuckle and orange essence that haunted his very dreams. He didn't like the singular notice he took of her graceful walk, her talent as a musician, her voice and luscious mouth.

He especially didn't like the way he had reacted tonight on the beach when she'd laughed out loud—such a husky, seductive sound. He'd felt amazingly lighthearted, rather than insulted, by her amusement at his predicament. He'd suddenly needed to touch her, and imprudently reached for her. He shouldn't have taken her hand. He'd caused her to jerk away—then fall in his lap.

And they'd kissed.

The hot coil in his gut torqued another revolution tighter, and he groaned.

Lauren stirred; her lashes fluttered. Before Dade could move, she was staring at him. Her expression altered quickly from sleepy bafflement to panic. "What—what are you doing!"

He felt like he'd been caught peeking through a hole in her shower stall. How ridiculous! He was doing nothing, really, but entering his room. She was dressed in perfectly decent sleeping attire. He hadn't touched her, not that it never crossed his mind. "I'm sorry," he murmured. "I saw the open door and decided it would be the quickest way to bed."

She lifted her arms across her breasts as though shielding herself from his lecherous view. "For the quickest way in, you weren't moving very fast!" she said in a sharp whisper.

"Seeing you sitting in the chair surprised me. I stopped." That was true enough. Of course, he didn't have to linger. "What are you doing there?" he asked, attempting to change the subject. "Aren't you cold?"

She visibly shivered. "I—wasn't when I sat down." Pushing up from the chair, she hurriedly turned her back on him and smoothed down her T-shirt. She was once again the stiff, prim Quinn. The woman who disliked him. Now, at least, he knew why. She believed he'd gotten her sister pregnant. Since he hadn't, he supposed they both had a bone to pick—with Joel. But that was water under the bridge.

"If you need another blanket, there's one in the closet," he offered, as she walked away from him.

"I'm fine." When she reached the foot of her bed, she faced him, her expression stony. "Good night—Dade." Her whisper was curt, her remark an undisguised request that he leave. It was evident she didn't want to be reminded of their kiss—or any active role she might have played.

In that at least, they could agree. For his part, he'd been reckless and stupid and would prefer to forget it, too. He dipped his head as a token of their unspoken pact never to speak of it. "Good night—Quinn," he whispered.

"What the hell is going on!"

Lauren heard Dade's angry charge from inside the nursery where she'd just changed Tina. She had decided to take her niece out on the patio for their accustomed afternoon bottle, but Dade's furious demand gave her second thoughts.

He'd gone into town with his guests for souvenir shopping and a farewell lunch. Lauren was disappointed that Joyce, Hadley and Ingrid were gone. She'd come to like them. On the other hand, she had no regrets about seeing Allegra go. Lauren didn't want to dwell on why. Just because the blonde was beautiful and didn't like the nanny—

"The hell, you say!"

Lauren lifted Tina from the changing table and headed for her patio door. She'd never heard Dade this angry. She peeked outside. Off in the distance she saw a column of black smoke, but she couldn't see what was burning. With a quick flick of her gaze, she spied Dade on the deck, towering over Goodberry. "What do you mean *another* outbreak? Have you lost your mind, man!"

Lauren didn't know what to do. Stay in the suite or go out. She didn't think Goodberry would be thrilled by an audience at his bawling-out. Then again, she'd never seen Goodberry look particularly terrified, or even bothered, when either Dade or Braga yelled at him.

Remembering she needed to get Tina's bottle, she elected to take the inside route to the kitchen, and hoped the bellowing would be over by the time she was ready to feed Tina.

A few minutes later, when she reached the Great Room's patio doors, Goodberry was entering. She whispered, "What's wrong?"

When Goodberry saw her, he swerved in her direction. "I've had to burn the rest of the guest room mattresses, miss."

Lauren was stunned by this bizarre news. "Why?"

"More mites, miss."

Lauren frowned in disbelief. "Fiber-eating?"

He nodded. "An extremely virulent strain."

"I've never heard of them."

Goodberry grinned. "My job is to know about such things, miss." He glanced from left to right then bent closer. "How are things going with you and your little niece? Are you feeling more secure about Master Dade as a father?"

Lauren felt a melancholy tug at her heart. "Yes," she said with a manufactured smile. "I'm finding him to be a very good father."

Goodberry beamed. "I'm glad you've had this opportunity to discover that on your own, miss. No amount of assurances can suffice over seeing for oneself, I've always said."

She nodded, holding onto her smile. "That's true. Had I not seen it with my own eyes, I would never have—been comfortable in my mind about it." Dade's fitness as Tina's father was the worst possible thing she could have discovered about Dade

Delacourte—billionaire genius. What chance did somebody like her have, gaining custody of an infant when she had a wealthy, caring father? "I'm so—happy."

"Goodberry!"

Lauren's head jerked up to see Dade standing in the patio entry. The manservant turned slowly, in his sedate, unruffled way. "Yes, sir?"

"What about the remaining beds?"

"No problem, sir."

Dade scowled. "Your bed and Braga's are fine?"

"And the nursery suite, sir. All miraculously spared."

"How fortunate," he said, his expression dubious.

Goodberry smiled. "I believe we've caught it all, sir."

"We have, have we?"

"Yes, indeed." Goodberry nodded. "I should be going now. There's the laundry."

"Are we going to burn it?"

Goodberry's smile remained courtly. "Heavens no, sir. Whatever would give you an idea like that?"

Dade eyed his man narrowly. "Maybe it's all the mattress smoke I've been inhaling. Which by the way, burning beds on the beach is illegal, and will no doubt cost me a hefty fine."

"In that case, may I make a suggestion, sir?"

"Why not. After burning all those beds, what's one little suggestion?"

"I wouldn't say anything about fiber-eating mites to the authorities."

"Why not?"

"We wouldn't want to cause a panic, would we, sir?"

"Or more likely, the beheading of one venerable, old psychopath?"

"You are wise beyond your years, Master Dade."

"You've made me *old* beyond my years." He looked as though he was going to say more, then changed his mind. With the wave of a hand, he barked, "Go on, Goodberry. I'll fire you later."

"Anything you say, sir."

Dade glowered at the servant as he walked serenely away. Once he'd disappeared, Dade shifted his glare to Lauren. "Do you know anything about this?"

She was stunned by the question. "Why would I want the beds burned?"

He raked both hands through his hair. "I don't know." He exhaled wearily and shook his head, as though trying to make sense of the nonsensical. "*Blast* it! I don't know." He turned and stalked away.

Lauren knew how he felt, because she felt every bit as despondent as he did. That morning, she'd breathed a sigh of relief when he left her room, satisfied their forced imprisonment was over.

Her property wasn't going up in smoke on the beach, but hours and hours of undisturbed sleep was disintegrating in that fire. The *last* thing she wanted was for Dade to share her suite—even for one more second! From the look of things, she had a sinking fear he'd be spending a *lot* of seconds in there.

A week passed. For Lauren, the nights ticked by in ponderous slow motion. She counted so many sheep she didn't think she'd ever be able to look a lamb chop in the eye again. She got hardly enough rest to keep from collapsing, facedown in her dinner each evening. Tonight was no different. She dragged herself to bed and lay there for hours, staring at the ceiling.

She had to stare at the ceiling, because if she lay on her side, she could see part of Dade's bed. See his face in the dim glow of the night-light. She didn't like looking at his face in repose. It reminded her too much of lying in his arms while he slept, of being held in his embrace.

To make matters worse, his kiss burned in her memory, refusing to be relegated to some deep, dank crevasse in her brain. She remembered how hot and passionate, yet tender his lips had felt against hers, and how her whole body had tingled with reaction. Heaving a disconcerted moan, she threw an arm over her eyes and redoubled her efforts to think about something *really* boring. *Dade Delacourte does not qualify,* the exhausted imp in her brain testily reminded. *You need sleep.*

A cry broke the stillness, and Lauren was immediately on her feet. Something was wrong with Tina! Single-mindedly she dashed into the room, running headlong into Dade as he made for the crib.

"Oh!" she exclaimed, reluctantly recording the hard contours of his chest, his pleasant scent, his arms coming around her, steadying her.

"I'm sorry." Their glances met, the impact was brief yet difficult for Lauren. His gray eyes shone like pearls in the weak light.

She twisted out of his embrace. "No harm done," she lied, refocusing her scattered wits on Tina.

"What do you think is wrong?" Dade asked as he joined Lauren beside the crib.

She felt inside Tina's plastic pants. "She's wet."

"Thank goodness."

Lauren lifted Tina from the bed, unable to keep from glancing his way. His expression showed true relief. This wasn't the kind of fatherly reaction that should cause her pain, but it did. Her hopes of getting custody of Tina seemed to be slipping further away.

Without comment she carried the fussing baby to the changing table and switched on the nearby lamp. Minutes later Tina wore a clean, dry diaper. Lauren picked her up, preparing to put her back in her crib.

"Let me have her."

She stilled, staring at him. "What?"

He lifted a shoulder in a casual shrug. "I'd like to rock her back to sleep."

Lauren frowned at him. "It's not necessary. She'll go right—"

"I know but..." He held out his arms. Goodness, the action looked so much like "Come to me, darling" she wanted to cry. Why did she have to read something so ridiculous in the mere extension of his arms? He wanted to hold his daughter, not her. She shook herself to get a grip on her swirling emotions.

"I suppose—if you insist." With the reluctance of a mother giving away her own flesh and blood, she handed Tina over. "I'll move the rocking chair in here."

"No need. I'd like to look out."

She glanced over her shoulder at him, wanting to say, *"I won't be able to sleep with you in there,"* but quickly faced the fact she wouldn't be able to sleep either way.

He followed her into her bedroom and settled in the chair before the patio doors. Lauren plopped heavily on the edge of her bed, debating whether to get in or sit and wait them out. Dade startled her when he glanced her way and smiled. "You don't need to watch me. I promise not to drop her."

She glanced away and sucked in a breath. "I—I'm not comfortable getting in bed with you there."

His silence made her shift her glance to his face. His smile had disappeared. "I see." He looked out the window. "You should have said that. I don't want to make you uncomfortable. I'll take the chair—"

"Don't bother. I'm not very—sleepy." She was brain dead, but how did she tell him *why* she couldn't sleep? Naturally that was unthinkable. It wasn't any more his fault he was sleeping in there than it was hers. Why make matters worse by whining—not to mention showing a certain troubling vulnerability around him. She waved off the idea. "You're fine. Pretend I'm not here."

He peered at her, his grin crooked, and without much humor. "Right."

When he turned away, she continued to survey him as he rocked. Every so often he glanced down at Tina, who watched him quietly. From time to time her eyelids drooped, then opened. Lauren had a feeling Tina resisted going to sleep, enjoying being in her father's arms. Unfortunately for Lauren, she knew the feeling. Being held in Dade's arms was *not* conducive to sleeping.

Dade smiled at Tina, whispering soft words Lauren couldn't quite hear. Her heart turned over with unruly affection for the handsome man, so obviously caring of his child. Spikey, who'd taken to sleeping under Dade's cot, pit-a-patted into the room and curled up beside the rocking chair.

Lauren studied the homey sight, facing a hard truth. Dade Delacourte was no rogue, no womanizing swine. She didn't know what had drawn him to Millie that night. But whatever it was, she now believed, had Dade known Millie was pregnant, he would have helped her. All the trouble was Millie's doing. She hadn't wanted his help. She'd had only revenge on her mind. And now Millie was gone, blithely unaware of the havoc and misery she'd caused her own sister.

No longer able to see Dade as a villain, Lauren murmured, "You didn't know the baby's mother was pregnant, did you?"

He peered her way. For a minute he only watched her in the darkness. Finally he shook his head. "No. I didn't."

"She didn't try to contact you before giving birth?" Millie had never mentioned it, but Lauren had had a feeling she didn't. That wouldn't have fit into her revenge scheme.

"Not that I'm aware of," he said, his smile holding no humor. "I'm not hard to find." After another quiet moment, he asked, "I wonder why she didn't want money?"

Lauren had asked herself the same question over and over. She couldn't tell Dade that, of course, but she did tell him her conclusion. "Maybe she valued her freedom more than money."

Dade's brow furrowed in thought. "And my enslavement?"

Lauren's cheeks went hot. "It's an awful way to put it."

"But it was her thinking?"

She shook her head, pretending not to know anything for sure. "It would seem so. Parenthood is a long-term—"

"A *long* term," he cut in, his expression serious. "A life sentence to be exact."

She was startled to hear him talk that way, after what she'd witnessed between him and Tina. "Is that the way you feel?" Hope surged in her heart. Maybe she'd been wrong! Maybe if she only asked—

"At first, yes," he said quietly, glancing at the baby. "Not now." His tone altered, softened, and he smiled. "She's my little girl." He peered at Lauren, his expression peculiarly speculative. "I love her, Miss Quinn."

Lauren experienced a crushing sadness. Dade wasn't the snake she'd believed him to be. She had to face the fact that her chances of getting custody of Tina were almost nil. Dade would be a wonderful father. He loved her. She could see it in his eyes, hear it in his voice.

Why, oh why, hadn't she come clean that first day? What if she'd told him the truth then? Maybe he would have given Tina up. But now? She wondered if being truthful at this late date might still salvage something?

Over the past week she'd vacillated a thousand times. But again and again she'd been too much of a coward to speak out. What if she told him the truth and he threw her out, and she lost Tina forever?

She wanted to be honest with him, but she lived with the terror of being ripped out of Tina's life. Until this moment, she'd held out a thread of hope Dade would do something, *anything*, to show he wasn't fit to raise a little girl. But that hope was now as dead as the mattress ashes washed out to sea.

She stared at him as he rocked, his gaze resting fondly on the baby, asleep in his arms.

What was she to do? Running away with Tina was rash and hazardous, but desperate people stole children from spouses or relatives every day. As she watched Dade and Tina together, her heart ached with such agony of loss and loneliness she could hardly keep from sobbing.

What could she do? If she revealed herself as the fake and liar she was, would he even consider giving her visiting rights? If the situation were reversed, would she do as much for him? It was doubtful.

She had so little to offer her niece. All she had was her small apartment, a lot of love and a salary that could barely afford a baby-sitter. Comparing what he had against what she had—and add to that her despicable behavior next to his—totally aboveboard—her chance at being a part of Tina's life was less than laughable.

The ferocity of her despair was frightening. Black desperation rushed over her like a killing flood.

Dare she grab Tina and run?

CHAPTER TEN

Now was her chance! Lauren never expected to be included on an outing to Sag Harbor, but this afternoon Dade, Goodberry and Braga all had things to do in town. Goodberry insisted Lauren go along—do a little sight-seeing in the village that, according to the manservant, had changed little in the past three centuries.

Goodberry dropped Dade off at an art gallery where a friend's work was being shown, then drove to an out-of-the-way grocery where he and Braga planned to do the marketing. When Lauren offered to help, Goodberry insisted she take Tina for a walk around the town. Perhaps stroll along the port, part of the picturesque shopping area.

Left to her own devices, Lauren set off with her niece. Tina was strapped to her back, cheerfully goo-gooing at anything and everything that caught her fancy along the old streets. Lauren had no idea who or what the baby might be talking to. Possibly the ancient trees shading fancy gingerbread houses of long-departed whaling captains. Or maybe Tina gab-gabbed at a chickadee on the wing, then a friendly passerby. Whatever Tina found to talk to, Lauren enjoyed the sweet sound, and hated the thought of spending a single day deprived of hearing it.

She wondered if there was a bus station in Sag Harbor. She knew what she contemplated was horrible. If she ran away with Tina, she would be a kidnapper and hunted by the police.

She glanced right and left. Off to one side, the harbor spread out along the shoreline. A forest of masts rose into the cloudless sky amid majestic profiles of motor yachts. On the inland side, restaurants and shops were nestled shoulder to shoulder along the winding streets. Beyond the town, nature predominated, and woodlands gave way to farms that stretched down to the sea.

Even in her anxiety and dismay, Lauren was impressed by the village, stunned to find such idyllic charm in the same hemisphere as an ''eat-or-be-eaten'' megalopolis like Manhattan. Back in Oklahoma, she'd pictured the New York state as nothing but an endless stretch of glass-and-steel high-rises and paved parking lots.

As she worried about what to do, she absently strolled and window-shopped. Beautiful scrimshaw and antiques, hand-crafted pottery and jewelry were everywhere, but she hardly noticed. When she realized she was ambling past the art gallery where Dade had gone, she hurried by, still unresolved about what to do. Maybe she should ask somebody where the bus station was—or the train station, if there was one.

She chewed the inside of her cheek. *Heavenly days! Lauren,* she shouted inwardly, *make up your mind! If you're going to run, you won't get a better chance than this!*

She decided the next person she passed, she'd ask. She spotted a woman coming toward her and bolstered her courage. ''Excuse me, ma'am?''

The middle-aged matron glanced her way. ''Yes?''

''I was wondering if you could tell me...'' She

hesitated. What was she doing? This was so wrong! No matter how much she wanted Tina, she couldn't steal her! She smiled wanly at the stranger and shook her head. "Never mind."

The woman smiled in return and continued on her way.

Hating herself for what she'd almost done, Lauren decided she might as well go back to the grocery store and wait for Goodberry and Braga. She couldn't run away, and she wasn't in the mood for window-shopping. At least at the market she could be of some help.

Pivoting around, she almost ran smack into a tall man. Luckily he was agile enough to quickly sidestep and avoid a head-on collision. "Whoa," he said with a chuckle.

She recognized that voice and jerked to look at the face. "Dade?"

One dark brow went up sharply. "That was close. Where was your mind?"

She shook her head, flustered and guilty. He'd been right behind her when she almost asked that woman about a train or bus station! "I must have been—daydreaming." She got herself together and gave him a stern look. "Why didn't you say something?"

"I thought about saying, 'Hi there,' but..." His grin was crooked and disquieting. "Let's just say, I prefer not to have my ego stomped in front of witnesses."

Her cheeks burned with the memory of the humiliating misunderstanding on the beach—and the kiss...

He gave her a searching look. "Is something wrong?"

She swallowed, but knew her cheeks were glowing.

"No," she lied. "I just—decided I'd had enough sight-seeing and was about to go back to the market."

"Not a good idea. You don't want to see Goodberry and Braga do the marketing. It's scary." He took her hand. "Trust me. You'd rather go down to the port and get a cup of coffee. It's a nice view. Especially at sunset."

She knew she should pull from his grasp, but some little imp took control of her better judgment and wouldn't allow her to jerk away. "Sunset? But it's only four."

He glanced her way, and grinned. "Don't panic, Quinn, I won't hold you captive until the sun goes down. I was just doing my bit for the Sag Harbor Chamber of Commerce."

She trudged beside him, too aware of his fingers, entwined with hers.

"Where were you going just then?" he asked.

She thought she detected an edge of suspicion in the question, but decided it was silly. Why would he be suspicious of his nanny? "I—I was merely wandering around."

He watched her for a heartbeat, then nodded. "It's a pretty town, isn't it?"

"Lovely." *So is your touch!* She blanched at that thought and decided she'd better get her mind off the warmth of his hand on hers—which she seemed to register most singularly—before she said something stupid. "Er, did you visit with your friend, the artist?"

He looked across at her. "Yes, she was there."

She. Of course! What made her think he would have a male artist friend. "Oh—that's nice," she murmured, wanting to keep the conversation moving until she could forget he held her hand. "Did you buy a piece of her artwork?"

"In a manner of speaking."

Lauren had no idea what that meant. "How do you buy art in a manner of speaking?" She wasn't sure she wanted to hear this, but it was better than blurting, *"I love it when you hold my hand! Kiss me!"* She cleared her throat, forcing herself on track. "You either buy art or you don't. Don't you?"

He motioned. "There's the coffee shop. They have ice cream, if you'd like some."

"Whatever," she murmured. She didn't care about anything but her need to have him let go of her hand! She could only take so much.

"Maybe Tina would like some." He glanced her way, his expression questioning.

Lauren didn't know if a baby Tina's age should have ice cream. "Only a taste," she guessed out loud.

"Okay." He grinned. "What kind do you want?" The outdoor café was half-filled with chatting, laughing tourists and townsfolk. Dade indicated a round wood-and-metal table with two chairs, in the shade of the bright yellow awning. The location had an excellent view of the bustling harbor.

"Vanilla," she said at last. Her wits had scattered, ever since Dade began dragging her around in his possessive grasp. It felt as though her entire mind had been sucked into contemplating his touch, leaving nothing for cogitating on other things—like ice cream. In her severely diminished mental state, vanilla was the only flavor she could think of.

He looked at her. "Vanilla?"

She shrugged, unable to help smiling at his dimpled incredulity. "I like vanilla. So sue me."

''I may have to.'' He released her fingers and went to the counter to place their order. Lauren inhaled shakily, trying to regain herself. As her brain began to function again, she registered that the air smelled of rich coffee and briny high tide.

After rubbing the feel of him off between her hands, she unfastened the carrier and drew Tina around to sit in her lap. As soon as the table appeared in front of Tina, the infant began to pound the surface with both hands. Lauren giggled. ''I can see you're going to be the lead drummer in your kindergarten band.''

Dade came back and seated himself across from her. It wasn't much of a distance, and his knees corralled hers. She could actually feel his radiant heat. A surge of excitement at his nearness made her furious with herself. Why was she so vulnerable to him? She could swear the man gave off some kind of crazy vibes that made her tingle all over.

''They'll bring our order,'' he said. ''You drink your coffee black, right?''

She nodded, surprised he'd noticed.

''What were we talking about?'' he asked.

Lauren had no idea. She didn't think it was how his touch affected her, but that was all she could come up with, so she shrugged.

Dade reached across the table and took Tina's hand between two fingers. ''I think you were asking how art could be bought in a manner of speaking, right?'' He glanced up from grinning at Tina to meet Lauren's eyes. The impact of his striking gaze and pleasant smile was hard on Lauren's heart. She managed to nod.

"I asked my friend to do a portrait of Tina, for her first birthday."

Lauren was stunned. This was certainly not what she'd expected. "Oh?" It was a lovely thought. A lovely, sensitive, fatherly thought. "How—sweet," she murmured, though she fought tears. Minutes ago, she had missed her best chance to run away with Tina. Not that she could have. But in the face of this news, her lack of action devastated her. He planned to have a portrait painted of Tina for her first birthday. How many fathers would think of such a dear gift? None but the most doting, she was sure.

Dade's smile remained intact, but something changed in his eyes. "Do you have a problem with that? Surely Dr. Wickerwhatever can't be against baby portraits."

She shook her head, unable to think of a single reason why any baby expert would find that a problem. "As long as she doesn't have to sit still for hours."

His rich laughter drifted over the conversations in the small café. Tina chirped and giggled, clearly delighting in the deep-throated ring of his voice. Tina wasn't the only female to find Dade's laughter appealing. Lauren couldn't help but notice that several women in the coffee shop turned, surveying him with approving glances.

"Making Tina sit still for five minutes would be cruel and unusual punishment for everyone involved," he said, then bent and kissed the baby's pudgy fingers. "The majority of the portrait will be from photographs," he added.

Lauren held her niece close, hating this man's prior claim, but no longer able to hate him. She tried hard to keep her expression pleasant, even as her whole world crumbled around her.

Dade woke abruptly. Sensing something was wrong, he swung off the cot and checked Tina's bed. She was there, sleeping peacefully. He frowned. Something woke him, but what? Curious, he peered into Lauren's room. In the dim moonlight he could see her rumpled bedcovers. But her bed was empty.

He glanced toward the bathroom. The door stood open; the light was off. He frowned. What was going on? Ever since that day a week ago in town, Dade's suspicions had been honed to a razor's edge. He felt it in his bones that Lauren Smith had had it in her mind to run away with Tina that day. He couldn't prove anything, but ever since he'd left instructions that either he or Goodberry be aware of her location at all times.

So where was she now? True, Tina was safe in her crib, but for all he knew Lauren could have packed her bag and gone out of the bedroom to another phone to call a cab. He decided to investigate, when something outside the window caught his attention.

It was Lauren. She was on the beach. Taking off her... "Clothes..." he whispered. She was going swimming in the nude? In the middle of the night? In the ocean? "That's not very bright, Miss Smith," he muttered.

Tina sighed in her sleep and wriggled, shifting her head from one side to the other. Dade moved away from the crib, but had difficulty taking his eyes off the figure on the beach. She stepped out of her panties and tossed them on her discarded T-shirt. He felt like a voyeur or a lust-crazed high school boy, ogling her as if she was an image in a girlie magazine.

"Blast!" he muttered, spinning away. Unfortunately the fact that she was out there, alone, gnawed at his gut. She shouldn't be out there by herself. That was stupid, especially at night. He didn't have much choice but to go get her. Halfway out the door, he realized she hadn't taken a towel, and pivoted around to grab one out of the bathroom. Then he headed down to the beach.

When he reached where her nightclothes were, he squinted out over the undulating sea, watching the waves break and rush toward shore. "Quinn!" he called. "Where are you?"

For a minute there was no answer, and he grew concerned. *"Quinn!"*

"What are you doing out here?"

He heard her, and shifted toward the sound. There she was, shoulder deep, about fifty feet from shore and off to his left. He loped in her direction along the edge of the surf. "Get out of there. Don't you know it's stupid and dangerous to swim in the ocean alone?"

"I couldn't sleep!"

"That's what warm milk is for. *Come here!*"

"I don't think so."

"Don't be stubborn. The undertow can be risky, and I don't feel like having to rescue you."

"Did y-you happen to notice my clothes out there?"

"You're cold." He held up the towel. "Come get warm."

"S-sure! You'd love that!"

"Don't make me come in after you."

"I'm naked!"

"I saw you undress from the window."

"You spied on me!"

He couldn't see her well, but he could make out the whites of her eyes. She was justly horrified. Maybe he shouldn't have been quite so truthful. "No, I didn't spy on you. I just—noticed."

"Yeah? W-well, how *long* did you notice?"

"I may owe a slight fine to the 'Stamp Out Oglers Society,'" he muttered.

"What?"

"I said, I promise I'll close my eyes." He walked into the surf until he was thigh deep in chilly water, then held the open towel above the waves. "Come here before you pass out from hypothermia."

"Your eyes aren't c-closed," she said. From this distance, he could hear her teeth chattering.

With a frown, he surveyed what he could see of her. She'd crossed her arms over her breasts and was glowering at him. He turned the other direction and closed his eyes. "Satisfied?"

"K-keep them closed!"

"They're glued. Now *move it!*"

"How g-gallant."

He kept quiet, but flapped the towel in a silent admonition.

"I—I'm coming," she said, sounding unconvinced.

Standing there with his eyes closed, Dade couldn't help recalling the sight of her nude body in the moonlight, so lithe, so supple. His gut tightened with desire, and he wished that for a moment at least he could put his doubts and suspicions about her aside. Take her into his arms and...

"I'm here."

The nearness of her voice startled him, and without thinking he glanced down. Her delicate beauty made his breath catch in his chest.

She gasped and tugged the towel from his hands, hurriedly wrapping it around her. She stared sharply at him, and even in the dim light her eyes blazed. "You *promised—*"

"I lied." His response instinctive and undeniable, he pulled her harshly, almost brutally against him. He was angry—both with himself and with her. *Why did he want her? She could well be his worst enemy!* His mouth captured hers hungrily, his kiss firm and furious.

He heard a plaintive whimper from her throat, and felt like a jerk. What was he doing? In the instant's hesitation before he could break off the kiss, her arms lifted to encircle his neck. Her lips opened, inviting, compelling!

With a groan of misgiving, but a need too strong to deny, he deepened the kiss and drew her more intimately against him. She raised up on tiptoe to better meet his lips, her body provoking, arousing. This time her response was anything but hesitant. She was all hot and sexy. All woman, ready and willing. He crushed her against him, his hands roaming, caressing. He cupped her hip and his body caught fire. He wanted her to be a part of him, wanted it more than anything. He wanted—wanted…

Are you nuts, man!

The woman was a fraud and a liar plotting a kidnapping, and you're kissing her? Even worse, the idiot you are, you like it—*too damn much!*

With a rough curse, he broke off the kiss and stumbled a step backward. He needed to put space between them—not only physical space, but emotional space. "That wasn't wise," he muttered, startled at how husky and winded he sounded.

"I didn't start it," she cried, sounding every bit as affected as he. "You—you kissed me!"

He ran a shaky hand through his hair and glared at her, making himself be harsh. The month was almost over. If she were going to make her move, it would be soon. "I was talking about the swim—alone—in the middle of the night. It was stupid and dangerous."

She swallowed hard, and with fumbling fingers adjusted her towel. She avoided looking him in the eye. *Damn him,* he didn't blame her.

"Yeah? Well..." she said, then cleared the quiver from her voice. "That's not the only stupid and dangerous thing that happened, tonight!" She swiveled away and marched past him, then seemed to have a thought and turned to stare at him. "I didn't know the rules for swimming in the ocean." She lifted her chin defiantly. "What's *your* excuse?"

Two more days! Lauren's mind spun with every conceivable scenario that would win her custody of Tina, if taken to court. Sadly they were all sweet fantasies with no possibility of coming true. She had nothing on her side that would tip the scales in her favor.

Dade Delacourte was Tina's father. He was caring—even devoted. He could afford to give her niece anything she would ever need. He wasn't a pervert—far from it. He was a kind, witty, generous man who cared about the environment, who took in stray mutts and whose kisses were miraculous, ethereal, almost too heavenly for this world. The memory of the touch and taste of his lips sang through her veins, burned in her heart, and she foolishly mourned the loss.

Suddenly weak from the memory, she slumped against the support for the steps that led to the deck. She'd gathered flowers alone, today. Dade and Tina had been so engrossed in a game of Lay On Daddy's Tummy and Stick Tiny Fingers In His Mouth and Giggle Lauren didn't have the heart to interrupt. To be honest, she found watching them together ironically soothing. She heaved a sigh. She was definitely losing her mind. She had two more days. Two days! For the past week, black gloom had been her constant companion. In two days Lauren would have no choice but to leave Tina and go back to Oklahoma empty-handed.

She couldn't even allow the thought to come full-blown to her mind. It was too painful. She must work up the courage to come clean with Dade, beg his forgiveness for the deception and ask him to allow Tina to be a part of her life. He wasn't mean or vindictive. Surely—

"Daddy's girl want to see the ocean?"

Lauren stilled and glanced up. She couldn't see Dade, but knew he'd come out on the patio with Tina. She slipped into the shadow beneath the stairs, not sure why. Maybe she just wanted to hear him be the daddy to her niece she knew he was. Adoring and adored.

She heard him laugh. "Da-da? Did you say Da-da?"

Tina jabbered something that made Dade chuckle. "Okay, maybe it wasn't Da-da, quite yet. I can wait."

Lauren loved the sound of his laugh. She bit her lip. She hated the thought of never seeing him again.

Or never hearing his deep, melodious laughter, or looking into those brilliant, pearl-gray eyes. Never again to detect his scent, watch him move, thrill to his dimpled grin. A lump formed in her throat.

It was true—something she hadn't wanted to face. She had fallen hopelessly in love with Dade Delacourte. He was a fine man who'd somehow made one mistake with Millie. A deviation from the norm of his world, she was sure. But a damaging one, for her at least—for it had brought her to this strange place, made her fall in love with a darling baby girl and a marvelous man, only to be ripped away...

"Master Dade," Goodberry said, interrupting her thoughts. "I must say this, sir."

"You look so serious, man." Dade's voice was rich with laughter. "Spit it out. Surely not more mattress burnings."

"No, sir. I want to express my admiration for you—for how you've taken on Joel's child, never letting on Tina is really your twin brother's baby. I know it was he who lied to the unfortunate woman, told her his name was Dade, to avoid—"

"*Goodberry,*" Dade cut in. Lauren could hear his footsteps as he moved to the railing. She ducked into the deep shade, perplexed by what Goodberry said. Her brain was having a hard time computing it. What did he mean? Who was Joel?

After a moment, she could hear Dade walk away from the railing. "Good, I don't see her."

"Her? Oh, she's out picking flowers. I'd forgotten."

"Goodberry, as far as the world is concerned, Tina is *my* daughter. Joel had his troubles, as we both know. I should have tried to help him. I didn't. That's why I feel the responsibility for this child is as much mine as his. *Never* mention it, again.''

''Of course, sir,'' Goodberry said quietly. ''I only felt you should know how proud I am about what you're doing. Naturally your secret is safe with me.''

''I should have realized you would guess.''

''Such a thoughtless act was out of character for you.''

''Thank you, Goodberry.'' Dade sounded strangely melancholy. ''But there are moments when my character might shock you. At least lately.''

''Excuse me?''

''Nothing. Never mind.''

Tina whimpered.

''Should I take the little miss, sir. I think she needs changing,'' Goodberry asked.

''Don't be silly, man. I can change a baby with one hand tied behind my back.''

''I shouldn't try it, sir.''

Dade laughed. ''It's a joke, old man. Don't be so serious.''

''Yes, sir. If you say so, sir.''

''That's better. Now if you'll excuse us, Tina and I have a date with a diaper.''

The squeak of redwood died away as Goodberry and Dade reentered the house. Lauren remained crouched in the shadows, hardly breathing. She was in such a state of shock she felt like she'd been doused with a bucket of ice water. What had she just overheard?

It sounded as though somebody named *Joel* was Tina's father. This somebody was Dade's twin brother—no doubt an identical twin—who lied about his name on occasion, calling himself Dade. And on these occasions, this Joel—who had "problems"—went around recklessly impregnating…

Of course! Of course! That would explain everything! Lauren sank to the sand, so weak from the revelation she couldn't support her own weight. Tears of joy filled her eyes.

Dade had no more claim on Tina than she did!

CHAPTER ELEVEN

ARMED with her exciting discovery, Lauren phoned her lawyer from her suite. She was so elated she could hardly talk, but finally got it all out.

"Well, what do you think, Mr. O'Conner?" she asked breathlessly.

There was a long pause on the line. "Legally, Miss Smith," the lawyer began solemnly, "even if all this is true, Mr. Delacourte has still been named the child's father on the birth certificate. And if this Joel is an identical twin, any DNA test would be inconclusive, I'm afraid." He paused to let his bad news soak in. "Since you have been unable to find any evidence that would prove him an unfit father, I see little hope in winning custody of the child."

After a few more questions, and equally depressing responses, Lauren hung up. Her hopes were dashed again and this time she feared the destruction was hopeless and permanent.

She slumped on her bed. Inside her head a voice nagged, *Dade is a good man, Lauren. Tina would have advantages with him she could never have with you.*

Though that truth clawed gashes in her heart, she had to face it once and for all. She could never legally win Tina, even if she could afford to fight Dade in court. It was clear from what she'd seen and heard this month, Dade had no intention of letting Tina go. With his patents bringing in a fortune, he could choose the hours he worked, and would never have to slave all day at a job the way she would—leaving Tina in the care of baby-sitters, which she could hardly afford.

Sick at heart, Lauren decided she must tell Dade the whole truth. She could only pray that he would allow her into Tina's life on occasion. With an infinitely sorrowful spirit, she fell back on the bed. "Tonight, after Tina's in bed," she vowed, tears sliding down her face, "I must *stop* being a coward and tell him."

Dade went to his den, but didn't feel like working. There wasn't anything that needed his immediate attention. He'd checked the faxes and e-mails. Nothing urgent. Hadley had everything running smoothly at Delacourte Industries. He didn't know why he was so uneasy.

If he were to face the truth, he wasn't worried about work at all. It was just a convenient evasion of what really bothered him and kept him awake. The trouble was Lauren. He'd spent so much time concentrating on mistrusting her, thinking her menacing and conniving, yet he was so damnably attracted to her. He wanted to run outside and roar out his frustrations.

Every time he looked at her, he felt a mixture of attraction and hesitancy, of fondness and resentment. He'd never experienced such a confusion of emotions in his life. He was beginning to fear for his sanity.

A soft knock at his door brought his glance up from an absentminded perusal of a balance sheet. "Come in?"

He was surprised to see Lauren standing there,

looking very serious. He studied her warily. "Is something wrong with Tina?"

She shook her head. "May I come in?"

He lifted a hand, motioning her forward. "Of course."

She came to stand before his oak desk. Somehow he sensed they were separated by much more than an antique piece of furniture. Concern lined her pretty face. She fidgeted, brushing a stray strand of hair behind her ear. He waited.

"I—I—I need to tell you something."

He watched her chew her lower lip, and experienced a twinge of foreboding. "Go ahead, Quinn."

"First—my name isn't Quinn. It's Smith. I'm—I'm Tina's aunt."

His nerves tightened and he stared. She was admitting it? He hadn't expected this. He eyed her levelly, wondering what she was up to. "I know—Lauren," he said softly.

Intense astonishment marked her pale face. "You—know?"

He nodded.

"Goodberry?"

"No. The agency wrote to apologize when they found out Quinn never showed up."

"But—then—why didn't you…?"

"That was Goodberry's doing." He pushed up from the desk and moved toward her. She looked like she might faint. "Here, take a seat."

Without hesitation, she sank into the chair he offered. "Goodberry asked you not to throw me out?"

Dade cocked a hip on his desk. "He seemed to think you were being honest about wanting to make sure Tina was okay. He asked me to give you the benefit of the doubt.''

She watched him with huge, liquid eyes. ''Oh...''

He crossed his arms before him. ''I thought you were going to steal her.'' He said nothing more, wanting to observe her reaction.

She blinked several times, and straightened her shoulders. He couldn't tell if she was trying to compose herself after being exposed or if she was merely uneasy in the face of his reproachful stare.

''I'm going back to Oklahoma,'' she said in a whisper.

He was too surprised by her declaration to do more than nod.

''I have a life there and—and I should get back to it.''

He frowned, trying to assimilate this new twist. ''Oh?'' He had no idea why he felt a rush of anger. Isn't this exactly what he wanted? Exactly why he'd given her the three weeks? So that she would go away quietly?

''I also know you're not Tina's father. You're her uncle.''

He stared, wordless. He knew Goodberry wouldn't have told. ''What makes you think that?'' he asked.

''All right, don't admit it.'' She heaved a sigh. ''It doesn't matter.''

He frowned, puzzled by her abrupt capitulation.

''But we both know, I have as much right to Tina as you. This past month, I've seen how much you love her. I also know you can give her—everything.'' She stopped, swallowed, then lifted her chin. ''To make a long story short—Tina will be better off with you.''

A strange, unexpected fury rose inside him. In his mind's eye, Dade saw a graphic rerun of his mother's desertion, recalling her using Lauren's exact words—"...be better off with you..." His mother had said that detestable phrase to Dade's father before she'd disappeared out of their lives.

So many people today just walked away from responsibility—as though it were yesterday's newspaper—leaving broken families and broken hearts in their wake. Dade had dealt with it by burying himself in his studies, but Joel had never gotten over it. He'd spent his life searching for something to fill that emptiness. Wreaking more havoc, and never finding what his mother's desertion had taken from him.

Suddenly overcome with rage, he wanted to toss Lauren out bodily, but he forced himself to remain outwardly placid. "How kind of you for leaving Tina in my care. Allow me to buy your plane ticket to start you on your way." Though his tone remained calm, he fumed inside. Lauren Smith was just like her sister, after all! She'd got bored and now she planned to run off—back to her established, uninterrupted life!

He'd actually believed Lauren cared about Tina. But here she was, slinking away, handing off responsibility, just as his mother had done when he and Joel were little more than infants themselves.

With a great wave of unexpected grief, he realized he would have had more respect for Lauren if she really had tried to steal Tina. He couldn't help but see the irony, and smiled cynically. "Would tonight be soon enough for you?"

She seemed alarmed for some reason. "Tonight?"

He stood up, retracing his steps around his desk to

sit in his leather chair. "I'll have Goodberry make the arrangements. He'll be happy to drive you to Islip."

"Islip?" Her voice was small, almost too quiet to hear.

"It's an airport."

"Oh..."

He picked up the phone and reached for the intercom button.

"But..."

He paused, ruling his anger with mighty self-control. "Did you say something?"

Her mouth worked for a moment before she managed to form words. "I hope you allow me to visit Tina—from time to time."

He gritted his teeth. Thin-lipped and barely under control he turned back to the phone. "I don't think I can allow that." Tina had been abandoned enough in her young life. Getting to know Lauren simply to have her walk away when the mood struck would only harm her.

"But, don't you think—"

"*No.*" He jerked his head toward the door. "I suggest you pack. Goodberry will help you with your bags. Just ring for him when you're ready."

She sat motionless as Dade told Goodberry she was leaving. When he peered her way, she seemed to wake from a daze and stood, looking shaky. "But, Dade..."

"Goodbye, Miss Smith." He shuffled papers, pretending to be absorbed in his work, but his throat burned and he felt like he was choking.

Unable to stop himself, he shot one last glance her way. She walked out of his world as stiffly as she'd walked in. When the door clicked shut behind her, he glared unseeing at his desk. He felt a twitching in his cheek and realized he'd clenched his jaws so tightly the muscle had gone into a spasm.

"*Hell!*" he muttered. His rage was illogical. The last thing he wanted was a custody fight, but Miss Lauren Smith wasn't planning to give him one. She merely wanted to flit in and out of Tina's life at her whim. If the truth be told, the fishing guide who was with Dade in the wilds of Oregon during the critical time period of Millie's impregnation could have been called into court. His testimony would confirm that Dade couldn't be the father.

Blast! What was his problem? Where was this gut-wrenching fury coming from? He should be glad she was gone, elated she was giving Tina up without a whimper.

Was he a mental case?

The next afternoon, Dade rang and rang for Goodberry. After the fifth try when he didn't answer, Dade put Tina down for her nap and went in search of him.

"Goodberry?" he shouted as he rounded the corner into the servant's wing. "Have you gone deaf?"

"No, sir," Goodberry called from his bedroom.

The door stood ajar, so Dade burst in. "Then what's wrong? Did you fall and break your leg?"

What he saw confused him. Goodberry was packing his suitcase. "What's going on? We're not leaving until tomorrow."

"I'm leaving today, sir."

"What? Why?"

"I'm quitting, sir." Goodberry straightened and made stern eye contact.

"You're..." Dade stared. Goodberry had been with the family so long, the word "quitting" didn't even enter into any discussion they might have. Dade had set up a trust for the servant that would allow him to live comfortably during his retirement years. He loved him like an uncle. "You can't quit."

"I just did, sir." The older man turned away and began to lift a stack of summer pajamas from a bureau drawer.

"No, you didn't!" Dade wasn't computing this. It was too bizarre. People didn't quit jobs with him.

"I'm afraid so."

"But, why?" He felt strange. Like the world had keeled off its axis and was reeling out of orbit. "I don't understand."

Goodberry pressed the pajamas into the bag and closed the lid before he faced Dade. When he did, his expression was sad. "I've been with your family for most of your life and much of mine. I've been as proud of you as I've been disappointed with Joel. But..." His mouth quivered and he pursed his lips to recover his poise. "With the wisdom of Solomon, that sweet Lauren gave up her niece to you. Making the sacrifice broke her heart. You're as unfeeling as your brother ever was!"

Dade stared, broadsided by Goodberry's condemnation. "That's absurd!"

"Is it, sir? Do you suppose that's why she sobbed uncontrollably all the way to the airport? Because she was bored and had nothing better to do?"

Dade ground his teeth. "Are you quite through?"

"I've said all I ever intend to say, sir."

"You're not seriously quitting."

"Quite seriously." He jerked his bag from the bed.

"I'll send the limo back with a replacement chauffeur, tomorrow." He hurried out of the room, leaving Dade in his wake.

After a moment Dade regained himself and strode after his longtime friend. "Don't do this, Goodberry," he called, experiencing a gamut of conflicting emotions—misery, anger, confusion, dread. What was happening to his finely tuned world? "Trust me!" he shouted, a desperate attempt to keep Goodberry from walking out. "The woman doesn't want Tina. When will you face reality and stop being a meddling old fool?"

At the front door, Goodberry turned, his eyes glistening with sorrow and pity. "When you stop being a blind, young one, sir."

CHAPTER TWELVE

THE school year began at Thomas Jefferson Elementary as it did every other year. Lauren went through the motions, but it was difficult, with such a gaping hole in her heart.

Millie had finally called a week ago, deliriously happy. She assured Lauren she was "so close" to getting a part in a situation comedy. She was sure, *this time,* her dreams of fame would become a reality. Any doubts Lauren might have harbored, she kept to herself. Millie wouldn't hear her, anyway. Wouldn't believe anything that smacked of uncertainty or skepticism. Lauren wished her sister luck, but felt a stab of pity—hoping Millie wouldn't squander her life grabbing for a star that was simply too lofty to reach.

In the whole half-hour conversation, Millie never mentioned Tina. How typical of Millie, Lauren thought, since not even an hour passed when Tina didn't dominate her own thoughts. She wondered how her niece was, if she'd changed much. If she remembered Lauren at all.

As torturous as missing Tina was, Lauren's wretched, foolish love for Dade ripped at her soul. She longed for the man who had kissed her so tenderly, whose laughter was like sunshine after a storm. But he hated her, loathed her. She'd written to him, pouring out her heart, asking forgiveness for her deception and pleading once again to be allowed into Tina's life, but her letter had gone unanswered.

She had no idea what horrible thing she had done to make him hate her so—unless it was simply his fear that if he allowed Lauren into Tina's life, she might become too attached and decide to try to take Tina away. She could understand such vehement, protective instincts where Tina was concerned. Still, the insight was agonizing.

She sucked in a tired breath, sweeping a stray wisp of hair behind her ear. The Parent Teacher Association meeting was in full swing, and she was next on the podium.

"Here is our Computers For Kids In The Classroom chairman for this year, Miss Lauren Smith."

Amid polite clapping from the school's concerned parents, she walked up the four steps that led to the auditorium's modest stage. Though her heart wasn't in it, Lauren smiled at the one hundred gathered parents, and flipped through her notebook to locate the proposals for moneymaking projects.

The applause died down, and she took a breath. "Ladies and gentlemen, as you know, every year we put on several activities—carnivals, contests, drawings—to raise money that will enable the PTA to buy additional computers for the children..."

She heard a noise, as though someone were joining her on stage. She flicked a glance toward the sound, and froze. A gorgeous man holding a precious baby was mounting the steps.

Speechless, Lauren could only stare. Was she hallucinating? Every dream she'd dreamed in the past two months had been filled with this very image!

The phantom Dade proved to be a solid reality when he placed an arm around her, drawing her close.

"Excuse me, Miss Smith," he said with a polite smile, then turned to face the audience. "I believe I can help get those computers. You see, I've come to steal away one very special teacher, and I hope to win the school's forgiveness with a generous donation."

He glanced back at Lauren. "I hope this special teacher can forgive me for being a blind fool. You see—I love her. I've loved her since the first minute she walked into my life." His smile grew melancholy, and Lauren could only gape, confused. Doubting her sanity and her hearing.

"Being a hardheaded fool, I had to find out the hard way—by missing her so badly it caused me physical pain." He faced the microphone. "I'm asking this teacher to come to New York and visit her niece. And one day, I hope she will agree to stay..." He glanced at Lauren, whispering, "And agree to be Tina's mother."

With a light kiss on her lips, he murmured, "And my wife."

Lauren felt light-headed, unsteady, so stunned she could only stare at his wonderful face, at the shimmer of emotion in his gaze.

A murmuring began in the audience. The sound rose and rose until the audience applauded and whooped in a standing ovation. The fanfare snapped Lauren from her stupor, and she flicked a gaze over the cheering, grinning faces.

"Lauren," Dade said softly. "I just proposed marriage. I wouldn't blame you if you never spoke to me again, but—"

"Would tomorrow be too soon?" she cried, feeling fluttery and dizzy and ecstatic.

His stunned expression was the most beautiful sight

she'd ever seen—matched only by Tina's innocent smile. Suddenly there were no shadows across her soul. She was wildly happy, fully alive.

Hugging him and the baby to her, she kissed his lips. Shivers of delight raced through her, heating her blood. "I love you so much," she murmured through a sigh.

He made a guttural sound, part growl, part sigh, part laugh. "Here, hold our daughter for a minute, darling." He presented Lauren with the second great gift of the day. She gladly accepted her precious niece, then found them both whisked into his arms.

Amid raucous applause and good-natured laughter, Dade carried his women off the stage. He swept them down the center aisle toward the back of the auditorium. Goodberry stood by the door, his round, sweet face beaming.

Not many days later, Owasso's entire school system was presented with new computers—ad infinitum. Miss Lauren Smith became Mrs. Dade Delacourte, and Tina's mama.

In due course the loving couple also became the parents of Michael and Kimberly and Stephen Delacourte, who had their mother's eyes and their daddy's dimpled smile.